SEX MACHINE

MARIE FORCE

Sex Machine
By: Marie Force
Published by HTJB, Inc.
Copyright 2016. HTJB, Inc.
Cover Design: Kristina Brinton
E-book Layout: E-book Formatting Fairies
ISBN: 978-1942295846

marieforce.com

The best way to stay in touch is to subscribe to my newsletter. Go to marieforce.com and subscribe in the box on the top of the screen that asks for your name and email. If you don't hear from me regularly, please check your spam filter and set up your email to allow my messages through to you so you never miss a new book, a chance to win great prizes or a possible appearance in your area.

CHAPTER ONE

Honey

"I want you to fuck me." I'm proud of the fact that I never blink as I stare into the baby blues of the man I just blatantly propositioned. In public, no less.

Blake Dempsey chokes on a mouthful of beer, his eyes watering as beer meets lungs in an unholy alliance.

For the first time since I walked into the dark, dank bar, my resolve begins to waver as I question the wisdom of this mission. But if I don't take the bull by the horns, literally, I might never know why everyone else makes such a big freaking deal about sex. My best friend, Lauren, has assured me that our old friend Blake Dempsey is the answer to my "problem," and she speaks from experience.

Tentatively, I pat him on the back, hoping to get him breathing again so we can get back to our conversation, such as it is. Let's face it —he's no use to me dead.

As he continues to hack beer out of his airway, people begin to take notice of us, which is the exact opposite of what I wanted. I'd planned to come into the dive bar where Blake has his end-of-the-day beer at exactly six thirty every night before heading home—alone—make my proposition and walk out of there with him.

I hadn't counted on him choking on his beer or having the eyes of every man in the place on me as I wait for him to recover and give me an answer. What if he says no? Men never say no to Honey Carmichael, which is part of my problem. I have a reputation for attracting them like bees to... well, honey. But I've never been tempted to keep one of them, thus my well-earned reputation as a love 'em and leave 'em kind of gal, even if that's never been my goal. No, I want one I can keep. Eventually. Until I find him, here I am with my hands on the bull's horns.

My dear sweet Gran used to say it's not my fault that I was blessed with thick honey-blonde hair, soulful brown eyes and breasts that have gotten me more attention than I ever wanted since high school. Not to mention the long legs that somehow manage to stay tanned year round and an ass that an ex-boyfriend once referred to as a work of art. I'll never deny I've had more than my share of attention from men.

The one thing I've never had is a decent orgasm with a man, which is why I'm still alone at almost thirty. I'd rather be alone than settle for a man who doesn't do it for me. But the curiosity about what I've been missing out on has brought me to tonight's mission, which is beginning to feel ill-fated.

Blake finally quits sputtering long enough to look up at me with eyes still watery from coughing. "You wanna run that by me again?"

"You heard me right the first time." I hold his steady gaze while trying not to give away my nervousness by fidgeting.

His steely blue eyes seem to look right through me, as if searching for the truth behind my blatant invitation. Despite the steel in his eyes, I also see sadness that makes me want to wrap my arms around him and tell him everything will be okay even if I have no way to be sure of that. Wishing I could make it better for him is the second reason I let Lauren talk me into propositioning him. As he runs his fingers through a short crop of dirty-blond hair, I can see his entire torso ripple with muscles under the tight T-shirt he wore to work.

My mouth waters at the thought of all those muscles wrapped

around me. I lick my lips as my nipples stand up to take notice and my pussy clenches in anticipation. From what I'm told by a reliable source named Lauren, Blake has the biggest cock in town and knows how to use it. That thought causes the throbbing between my legs to intensify. When desperate times call for desperate measures, I believe in hiring the best man for the job. And these are most definitely desperate times.

"What brought this on?" His sexy drawl and the relaxed way he occupies the barstool belie the intensity of his stare. To look at him, filthy from a day of hard, physical labor, one might dismiss him as just another working man.

One would be mistaken.

Blake runs the most successful construction and renovation business in the area, and judging by his grimy appearance, he works as hard as the many men he employs. On him, the grime only makes him more appealing.

"Did you finally run out of guys to fuck in this town? No one left but me?"

I can't deny that I've probably had a few too many one-night stands as I searched for the elusive *something* that has other women waxing poetic about the act. To me, it's nothing special, two bodies coming together to expend some energy. Big deal. I've never understood what all the hoopla is about, a sentiment I recently shared with Lauren. After she finished laughing at me, Lauren said, "If you want to know what the hoopla is about, you need to fuck Blake Dempsey."

Lauren ought to know. She was with him years ago and declared him an absolute *machine* in bed. Lauren assures me that doing the deed with Blake will result in nonstop orgasms and pleasure unlike anything I can possibly imagine. "One night with him," Lauren said, "and you won't wonder anymore."

"You wouldn't care?" I asked my friend.

Lauren shrugged. "It was just sex between us. That's all he's capable of. Everyone knows that. A girl would be a fool to fall for him, so I took what I could get, and when it was over, it was over. It was a long time ago. Have at him and The Cock."

Even though I've known Blake all my life and have never once considered him boyfriend material—mostly because my best friend had sex with him ages ago—I'm desperate enough to know what I've been missing out on to walk into a bar and utter a sentence that no doubt has my dear, sweet Gran rolling in her grave.

I can't think about what Gran would have to say about me unashamedly propositioning a man. All I can think about since the conversation with Lauren a week ago are the words "machine" and "nonstop orgasms." The best orgasms I've ever had are the ones I've given myself, thus my need for Blake and his legendary cock.

"Are you gonna answer the question?"

I snap out of the fog to realize I've been staring at him while he waits for me to answer him. "What was the question again?"

"Did you run out of other guys to fuck? Is it down to me?"

I hold back a wince at his judgmental tone. I'm not proud of the number of men I've test-driven, seeking the hoopla. "What do you care?"

"I don't." It's a well-known fact that Blake Dempsey doesn't care much about anything other than his family, his business, the people who work for him and a few select friends, of which I'm one, or I was until about five minutes ago anyway. He shrugs as he drains the beer bottle and puts it on the bar next to a ten-dollar bill. "It's your business, not mine."

When he stands to his full six-foot-three-inch height and looks down at me, I nearly swallow my tongue. My nipples stretch against the confines of my bra and tank top, as if they're reaching for him. I hold my breath, waiting to see what he will do.

He brings his head down close to my ear. "Follow me home." His tone is gruff and sexy and authoritative.

I shiver as my heated core weeps in anticipation. My eyes travel from broad shoulders to lean hips and below, where the outline of that legendary cock has me licking my lips once again. Soft, faded denim hugs him in all the right places, and it's all I can do to refrain from reaching for the button and giving it a tug to get things started.

My mouth waters as I picture his big cock springing free of his clothes, ripe for my mouth, my pussy and anywhere else he chooses to put it. *Wait. What?* No, not *that*, not with him. No way.

"Honey?"

Once again I shake off the sexual stupor and force myself to meet his gaze. If thinking about sex with him gets me this hot, I can't imagine what the actual deed might entail.

"Are you coming?"

Even though Lauren assured me he wouldn't say no, I'm still insecure enough to be surprised that he accepted my offer. *Oh my God*, I'm really going to have sex with Blake Dempsey. Resting a hand on his sculpted chest, I say, "Oh yeah, I'll be coming, and so will you, big boy." The cocky statement, exactly what he expects from me, covers the quaking going on inside.

A throbbing pulse in his chiseled jaw is the only sign of emotion in his otherwise blank expression as he takes me by the hand and heads for the door.

Mindless of the prying eyes of the other customers, I scramble to keep up with his long-legged stride.

"Where's your car?" he asks when we're outside in the fading sunlight.

Heat from the long summer day rolls off the blacktop in scorching waves, but I shiver from the almost predatory way he looks at me. "There." I point to my tiny silver car with the decal on the side hawking my photo studio.

"I'll wait for you." He drops my hand and stalks to his big black truck bearing his own company logo on the side. His long strides eat up the pavement. I watch him go, fascinated by the way his jeans hug his muscular ass. I can't wait to see if his ass looks as good naked as it does in denim. Who am I kidding? It'll look even better.

I order my quivering legs to *move*. They finally get the message, and I rush to my car, managing to drop my keys in the dusty dirt parking lot. I bend to get them and am scorched by awareness. As I stand up, I venture a glance at his truck and find him watching me intently, his entire focus on my ass. The quaking begins anew as I get into the car and fumble some more with the keys before managing to get the car started. At this rate, I'll need an insane asylum before I ever get what I want from Blake.

His truck leaves a cloud of dust in its wake as he pulls out of the parking lot onto Highway 90, heading out of downtown Marfa, Texas. The sun is a ball of fire in the sky as I follow him at a safe distance. The last thing I need is to smash into his back end because I'm such a nervous fool. It's not like I've never come on to a guy before. I have, once or twice. But even though we share mutual friends and have known each other forever, Blake has always been so remote and off-limits that it took all my courage to walk into that bar and say the line that Lauren and I rehearsed until I got it just right. My hands are trembling and sweaty as I reach for my phone.

"What'd he say?" Lauren asks when she picks up on the first ring.

"I'm following him home."

"To his *house*?"

"Yes."

"This is huge! He never takes women to his place." Lauren lets out a shrill squeal. "I'm so jealous!"

Instantly alarmed, I swerve before I right the car. "You said you didn't care!" I can't lose Lauren, the closest thing to family I have left. "I'll call it off right now if you don't want me to go with him."

"I'm not jealous about *him*. I'm jealous that you get to be with *The Cock*."

I swallow hard. "It can't be that different from all the others."

Lauren's dirty chuckle comes through the phone. "Oh, Honey... You have no idea what you're in for. Tomorrow, when you're walking bow-legged, remember I told you so."

A bead of sweat slides down my backbone. Propping the phone between my ear and shoulder, I turn the AC on high and follow the black truck as it hangs a left onto Antelope Hills Road. "You always did exaggerate, Lo."

Lauren snorts with laughter. "You'll know soon enough that I'm *not* exaggerating. Call me in the morning. I want every single detail. In fact, if you could take notes, that'd be great."

"Shut up."

"Honey..."

The unusual seriousness in Lauren's voice puts me immediately on guard. "What?"

"Ever since your Gran died, you've been looking for a place to call home again. It's not going to be with him. No matter what happens, don't forget that. Do you hear me?"

"I hear you."

Blake's story is well known around town. He blames himself for the car accident our senior year of high school that claimed the life of his girlfriend, Jordan Pullman, who was also a friend of mine and Lauren's. The loss of Jordan rocked our entire class, but no one more so than Blake. Even after the police ruled that the accident was the fault of the other driver, Blake continued to blame himself. He's kept his distance from people—especially women—ever since, throwing his considerable energy into his business. Occasionally, he takes a lover, but he never keeps her for more than a night.

My story is equally well known. Abandoned at the church when I was days old, Nora Carmichael, who never married, took me in and raised me as her own. Because Nora was in her early sixties when I came to live with her, I always called her "Gran." She died ten years ago when I was only twenty, leaving me to fend for myself in an unforgiving world. I've done okay, all things considered, but it's been a struggle.

"Call me in the morning?" Lauren says.

"I will."

"Remember: only sex."

"I gotcha."

"Did you use the 'I want you to fuck me' line?" Lauren asks. We debated a number of ice-breaking lines and settled on the most direct of the many choices.

"Sure did."

"I need to try that one on Garrett."

Poor Lauren has been lusting for years after Garrett McKinley, accountant to Blake's company and most of the other businesses in town, including mine. "What's stopping you?"

"Um, only the fact that he thinks I'm a brainless floozy."

"You're neither brainless nor a floozy. Look at what a booming business you've made of the flower shop. How can he think you're brainless?"

"Maybe because I act that way any time he's in the same ZIP code as me?"

"I still say you should hire him to do your books. Then he'll find out how full of brains you really are."

"Not happening. I wouldn't give him the satisfaction."

I watch Blake pull into a driveway a block in front of me. The door on a two-car garage goes up, and Blake pulls in. "I gotta go. We're at his house."

"Just sex," Lauren says one more time.

"I heard you the first ten times. Bye, Lo." Ending the call, I repeat Lauren's refrain. "Just sex." The last place in the world I'm going to find my home is in the arms of the most remote man I know. Determined to take this one night, and only this one night, with him and "The Cock"—a thought that makes me giggle nervously—I follow Blake's hand signal to pull into the empty half of the garage.

By the time I make it out of my car and into the laundry room that adjoins the garage, he's removed his work boots and stripped down to boxer briefs that hug his tight ass.

I stare at the muscles on his back that taper down to that most excellent butt—and wonder if we're going to get busy right here. I clear my throat to remind him I'm here.

He seems in no particular rush as he tosses his clothes into a front-loading washer, adds detergent and starts the cycle. Then, as if I'm not there, he goes into the kitchen.

I'm not sure if I'm supposed to follow him, but I do it anyway.

He hands me a piece of paper. "Tell them to send my usual and get whatever you want."

I somehow manage to tear my gaze from the most lickable male chest and ripped abs I've ever seen to glance at the print on the paper. I recognize the logo of Pizza Foundation. "They don't deliver."

"They do for me. I pay extra."

"I'm not hungry."

He shoots me a meaningful look. "I worked all day, and if I'm going to be expected to work all night, too, I need fuel—and so do you."

A burst of heat creeps from my chest to my face as the implications of his statement settle on me. *All night. Whoa.*

"Make the call. I'm going to grab a shower. There're drinks in the fridge. Help yourself."

For a long moment after he leaves the room, I stand motionless in the middle of a nicer-than-expected kitchen. What the hell am I doing here? Did I really go to the bar Blake Dempsey frequents and ask him to fuck me? "You've lost what's left of your mind, Honey Carmichael."

I could cut my losses and leave while he's in the shower. Sure, the few times a year that I run into Blake at the grocery store or post office or at the home of a mutual friend would be awkward from now on, but I can live with that if it means saving some face.

My cell phone chimes with a new text message that jostles me out of my temporary paralysis. Digging into my purse, I pull out my phone. From Lauren: *No matter what, don't chicken out. You'll be sorry forever if you do. Trust me on that!*

As always, Lauren's timing is impeccable. Sucking in a deep breath and releasing it, I call in the pizza order and then take a beer from the fridge. If there's ever been a time for liquid courage, this is surely it.

CHAPTER TWO

Blake

A girl walks into a bar and shocks the shit out of a guy... Not in a million years did I expect this day to turn out the way it did, with Honey at the bar asking me to fuck her.

I run a razor over my face, and then, thinking of Honey's flawless complexion, I do it again, though if this encounter goes all night, it won't matter. My beard grows back fast.

So Honey Carmichael has finally gotten around to me. It's taken long enough. Honey is the one girl from my childhood who never threw herself at me after I grew from a scrawny kid into a man with man-sized appetites. Rather, she's remained an enigma as she worked her way through several other guys in town.

I've wondered—more often than I'd ever admit to anyone—why she seems to date every guy *but* me. Is it because there's always been a spark of *something* between us, something potentially incendiary, or is it just me who feels that? Doesn't matter now, I decide, as I step out of the shower and grab a towel.

For once, I actually bother to run a comb through my hair and slap on some of the face lotion my mother gave me for Christmas. And with that, I've done three times as much to prepare for this evening with Honey than I have for any other woman in years.

Honey Carmichael.

As I think about the night ahead, my cock twitches in anticipation. Will she taste as sweet as she looks? Will her breasts be a perfect handful, or are they as big as they seem? What color are her nipples? And is the honey color of her hair the *real* color? I can't wait to find out.

With one last look in the mirror, I conclude that I'm as presentable as I ever am and head into the bedroom. Shit! The sheets! I can't remember the last time I changed the linen on my king-size bed. Moving quickly, I grab clean sheets off the closet shelf and make fast work of putting them on the bed. Then I pull on a pair of gym shorts and go out to see what trouble Honey has gotten into in my absence.

I find her nursing a beer and flipping through the photo album of my childhood that my mother gave me for Christmas.

Without looking up at me, Honey says, "You were an awfully cute little boy."

"You should know. You were there." I can't remember a time when I didn't know her.

"You were very mean and aloof back then."

That surprises me. "Was I?"

"Uh-huh. I used to go home and tell my Gran that you'd been mean to me."

I sit on the sofa, keeping a reasonable amount of space between us. I have to eat before I touch her, because once I start, I won't stop until the sun comes up. Thank God tomorrow is Saturday, and I've given my crews the weekend off after a month of seven-day workweeks. "I was *mean* to you? When?"

Honey lets out a delicate-sounding laugh that catches the attention of my restless cock. He can't wait to get in on this party. "You really don't remember, do you?"

"I'm afraid not."

"You used to chase me around the playground and pinch me until I cried."

"I did not!"

"Yes, you did."

"You're making that up."

"I am not! I think I remember who pinched me and made me cry."

"I'm sorry I made you cry."

"That's okay. It was a long time ago."

We share a smile that's full of nostalgia and promise, and it's all I can do to keep my hands to myself. The doorbell rings, saving me from pushing the photo album off her lap and getting an early start on the night's festivities.

I pay the delivery boy and carry the pizza box and bag to the kitchen, the smell making my mouth water. I'm always starving after a long day at work. I grab a beer from the fridge and pop it open. Honey appears at the door, looking hesitant and unsure of herself, bearing no resemblance whatsoever to the woman who boldly propositioned me an hour ago.

"This is all you got?" I ask of the small salad in the bag. "That's nowhere near enough."

"It's all I wanted."

"You're going to burn a *lot* of calories tonight." I love watching her face flame with color when I remind her of why she's at my house and what's going to happen after dinner. I get the feeling she's nowhere near as ballsy as she wants me to think she is after that blatant come-on at the bar. "That's okay. I'll share my pizza with you."

I flip open the lid to the thin-crust pepperoni and green-pepper pizza with extra sauce cooked well done. "Now that's a pie," I say as the delicious aromas fill the air.

"It does look good," she says wistfully. "I can't remember the last time I had pizza."

"Don't you like it?"

"I love it. That's the problem. Too fattening."

I take a long perusing glance at Honey's trim figure that curves in all the right places. "You can afford it."

"Not if I eat pizza every time I have a taste for it."

From the cabinet over the dishwasher, I get out two plates, putting three slices on mine and one on hers. Handing her the plate and a fork, I say, "You're going to need your strength, Honey Bunches of Oats."

"Nothing wrong with your self-confidence," she mutters, but I can tell she's amused by the nickname I've given her.

Laughing at her comment, I study the sweet blush that flames her cheeks, wondering why I've never noticed the way her face lights up when she's embarrassed. If I have my way, her face will be bright red all night long. I plan to embarrass the living hell out of her before I'm finished with her. While taking a swig of my beer, I keep my gaze fixed on her. "Tell me something, Honey Carmichael." I wait until I have her attention. "Why me? Why now?"

Honey

I wrestle with how I should answer his question. Do I dare tell him the truth? That I've heard he's a god in bed, and I'm dying to be with a real man who doesn't fumble his way through the act like a randy teenager getting laid for the first time? Or do I feign boredom and let him think he's one of the last remaining men in town who hasn't been favored with my attention when he's *far* from the last one standing? I've never gone near his friends Matt or Garrett, for example.

"Tell the truth, Honey," he says, seeming to read my thoughts.

Am I really so transparent? Or is he that perceptive? I put down my fork and blot my lips with a napkin. "I want to be with someone who knows what he's doing without having to be told." The words are out of my mouth before I consciously decide to go with the truth.

"And you think I know what I'm doing?"

"That's what I've heard."

He lets out a bark of laughter. "Why do guys get accused of kissing and telling when women are the ones who do all the talking?"

"We don't 'talk' so much as compare notes."

"Is that right? And what 'notes' have you gotten about me?"

"Just what I said. You know what you're doing."

Blake lets the beer bottle dangle between his fingers as he eyes me wolfishly. "You want to find out if it's true?"

I swallow hard and try not to blink as my entire body heats up. "Don't my actions thus far this evening speak for themselves?"

His grin is arrogant and sexy at the same time. "Eat your pizza."

"I'm not hungry." I'm too nervous to eat—not that I'd admit that to him. What had seemed like a brilliant idea an hour ago is becoming more and more ludicrous by the minute. I've known Blake all my life, and after tonight, every time I run into him around town I'll be forced to remember how I propositioned him, asking for sex like a common floozy. "I've never done this before." It's suddenly crucial that he know I've never blatantly propositioned another man the way I did him.

"Done what?"

"Asked a man to... you know..."

His eyes twinkle with amusement. "Fuck you?"

Does he have to toss my own words back at me? I push my chair back from the table and stand. "I made a mistake. I shouldn't have done this. I don't want you to think—"

He stands and moves quickly to stop me from heading for the door. Even though he's made of muscle and has at least seventy pounds on me, I don't feel threatened by him. Rather, his nearness makes my skin prickle with awareness. The light dusting of hair on his chest is darker than the hair on his head. I let my eyes roam hungrily over well-developed pectorals, to washboard abs and below to the tuft of dark hair that makes a path from his abdomen into the waistband of his shorts. I force my gaze back up to find him staring down at me.

His hands land on my hips, drawing me in closer to him, so close that our breath mingles and his lips hover perilously close to mine.

I can't help but notice how perfectly our bodies align, with my head landing just below his chin.

"Don't ever be embarrassed about asking for what you want," he says gruffly.

"Despite what I said to you in the bar, I don't want you to think I'm cheap."

"I could never think that, Honey. You're beautiful. I've always thought so."

"You have?"

He nods and touches the lightest of kisses to my lips.

I feel the impact of that kiss in every cell of my body. I arch into his embrace, wanting so much more.

Turning his attention to my neck, he feathers kisses in a trail of fire that make me whimper.

"Easy," he whispers. "I'll give you what you want, darlin'. We've got all night."

His words relax and inflame me at the same time. How is that possible?

"Touch me, Honey."

All at once, I realize my hands have been dangling awkwardly at my sides while he spins a magical web around us. I raise them to his back, my palms coasting over warm, smooth skin.

He gasps, and his hands drop to my bottom, tugging me in tight against the hard ridge of his erection.

As I make contact for the first time with "The Cock," I choke back a gasp of my own while he throbs against me. I yearn to touch him there, but hold back, not wanting to seem too eager.

He takes the decision away from me when he grasps my hand and brings it to rest on his pulsating member. "Did you hear about this, too?"

My mouth has gone totally dry as my fingers learn his length and girth. *Good God.* My pussy moistens in anticipation.

"Did you?" he asks again.

I nod and flatten my palm against him, working my way from root to tip and reveling in the twitch that jolts his tightly clenched jaw.

"What did they say?"

"I, um... They said it was big."

"Is it?"

"You know it is." How I manage to speak when his hands are digging into the flesh of my ass is anyone's guess.

"Is it the biggest you've ever felt?"

"Yes."

"Do you want it inside of you?"

"*Yes.* Oh, *yes.*" All worries of appearing wanton or cheap flee in a tsunami of need and desire that spreads from the palm of my hand to every pressure point on my body.

His breath against my ear makes me shiver. "Is your pussy wet just thinking about it?"

I nod, making him grin with satisfaction. With any other man, the arrogance would've been off-putting, but with him, somehow, it adds to his overwhelming appeal.

"We'll get to that," he says. "Eventually."

I want to moan and protest, but he takes my hand and leads me into his bedroom. "Is it true you never bring women here?"

The question stops him in his tracks. He turns to me and raises a brow. "Is there nothing you haven't already heard about me?"

I shrug even as I hope I haven't ruined the mood with one question too many. "I heard you don't bring women home as a rule."

"I don't."

"Why me? Why now?"

He smiles as I toss his words back at him. "Honey Carmichael asked me to fuck her. I couldn't take the hottest girl in town to a cheap motel."

The mortification returns in a hot blast as the reminder of my proposition mingles with an unexpected compliment. "Are you ever going to forget I said that?"

"Not in this lifetime—or the next."

"Great."

His brows waggle seductively as amusement dances in his normally somber eyes. It's nice to see him smile. "It will be, darlin'. I promise."

My legs quiver beneath me at the sensual overtones I hear in his gruffly spoken words.

His fingers find the hem of my tank top, drawing it up and over my head. When he encounters the lacy bra I wore with him in mind, his blue eyes darken with desire. The bra joins the tank top on the floor.

"Pink," he says, his gaze fixed on my breasts.

"What is?"

"Your nipples." He circles each of them with his index fingers. "I wondered what color they'd be. Now I know."

"You wondered about me? Before tonight?"

Nodding, he tugs on the button to my denim shorts and has them off me so quickly, I wobble and am forced to grip his shoulders to keep from falling off my three-inch heels.

The sheer thong that matches the bra is damp from the verbal sparring that led to this moment. "What else did you wonder about?"

"Whether your hair down here matched your name the way your other hair does." He cups my mound, dipping his middle finger between my labia and dragging the fabric over my inflamed pussy. "Which it does."

I moan and tighten my grip on his shoulders.

"So wet," he whispers. "And we haven't even done anything yet."

I'll never survive this. I wanted to know what all the hoopla was about, but nothing could've prepared me for Blake Dempsey's special brand of intense sexuality. If anyone had asked me before tonight if I had experienced real desire, I would've said of course I have. But I would've been wrong. *This* is real desire. For the first time in my life, I get it. If this is what it's like for them, I get why other women go crazy over sex.

He keeps up the back-and-forth motion of his fingers until I'm answering his strokes with the rhythmic movement of my hips.

"Don't stop." I'm on the verge of something big and powerful.

"Wouldn't dream of it." Wrapping his free arm around my waist, he tugs me closer and bends his head to suck hard on my nipple.

I grasp a handful of his hair to keep him there while I rock against his hand as my orgasm builds and builds and finally bursts forth in wave after exquisite wave of pleasure unlike anything I've ever experienced with a man. One orgasm and he's already different from every other guy I've been with. The realization settles on me as I come back to reality to discover he's lowered me to his bed and is hovering above me.

His busy fingers continue to stroke and soothe my pussy through the aftershocks. "Beautiful," he says softly, making me blush ferociously as I imagine how uninhibited I must've appeared in the throes of release.

The tension in his jaw seems to have multiplied as he guided me through the cataclysmic release.

I reach up to caress his face and watch the tension drain away under my touch.

He cups my breast and stares at my nipple, his eyes hot with desire as he dips his head to touch his tongue to my flesh. "Delicious." He holds me still for the heat of his mouth as he suckles first one and then the other nipple, all the while continuing to stroke between my legs with his other hand. "God, you're sweet as honey. I always knew you would be."

He always knew? I run my hands over his muscular back until I reach the waistband to his shorts. Burning with curiosity, I push my hands inside to clutch his firm ass. That draws a tortured groan from him as he sucks hard on my right nipple.

I cry out and squeeze his ass again.

"Touch me, Honey." His tone has gone from seductive a short time ago to pleading now. "Touch me before I die from wanting you to."

I know exactly what part of him he wants me to touch, and if I had any doubt, he lifts to give me room to move my hand from the back of his shorts to the front. Starting at the broad base, I try in vain to wrap my hand around his thick girth.

Oh my God. I stroke my way up, up, *up* the hard, pulsing shaft. *Sweet Jesus, he's huge.*

As if I haven't just experienced the most explosive orgasm of my life, my clit burns and throbs with renewed anticipation. The muscles in my thighs tighten, seeking relief from the relentless need building again.

While I explore his length, Blake goes still above me. His eyes are closed, and his Adam's apple bobs in his throat. That I'm having such an effect on him is a powerful aphrodisiac, not that I need any help in the arousal department. I've never been more turned on.

Finally, I reach the tip and run my thumb through the fluid that has gathered there. I let my thumb dip into the slit at the top, drawing a deep moan from him.

Suddenly, it isn't enough to feel "The Cock." I want to see it, too. I release him, which results in another tortured groan, and ease his shorts down over his hips. "Get on your back."

"Wait, I want to—"

"On your back," I say more forcefully.

"Whatever the lady wants."

After he shifts into position, I free his cock from his shorts. My eyes go wide, and my mouth falls open.

"Like what you see?" he asks, watching my every move.

I nod even as another trickle of anxiety works its way down my spine. Other lovers have commented on how small and tight I am. What if he doesn't fit inside me?

He tugs on the strand of my hair that has landed on his chest, drawing my attention to his face. "Don't stress. We'll take it nice and slow."

I probably ought to be concerned about how well he reads my thoughts, but I'm too focused on the male buffet laid out before me, awaiting my next move. I bend my head to press light kisses to his chest, focusing on the dark disks of his nipples, teasing them with my lips and tongue until they stand up at attention. All the while, I drag my breasts over his rippling stomach.

Working my way down, I kiss, nip and lick a trail to his belly button. He smells like soap and sunshine and hard, muscular man. Dropping my tongue into the indent of his belly button, I'm surprised when his grip on my hair tightens and he sucks in a sharp deep breath. Full of my own power, I wrap my hand around his cock and lift it off his stomach.

Before this, before him, I'd had no idea that penises were made this big. I stick out my tongue and touch it to the slick tip, teasing the slit by darting in and out.

"*Fuck*," he moans. "Honey... *God*." His eyes are closed, his head thrown back, and once again, his Adam's apple is prominent as it moves in his throat.

I open my mouth as wide as I can and wrap my lips around the broad head of his cock, sucking and pulling on the tender flesh and lashing him with my tongue while continuing to stroke him with my hand. Forcing another inch into my mouth, I moan in frustration when I realize I can't possibly take all of him.

The vibration of my moan against his shaft leads to a sharp cry from him, which only fuels my determination to bring him as much pleasure as I possibly can. He's always so serious and solemn. I want to make him forget his terrible burden, even if just for a little while.

I draw back and run my tongue from tip to root, focusing on the sac that is drawn up tight against his scrotum. My tongue outlines first one testicle and then the other. With my hands on his thighs, I urge him to raise and spread his legs.

The instant my tongue makes contact with the sensitive skin under his sac, he explodes, sending streams of semen shooting onto his chest and abdomen.

I grip him tighter with my hand, stroking him as hard as I dare and drawing another deep groan from him.

"Holy shit," he whispers, gasping in the aftermath.

I flash him a victorious smile and use my hand to spread his hot seed over his ripped abs.

"Honey! Fuck!" His recently satisfied cock is as hard as it was before he came and makes its presence known by pulsing between my breasts. I slide them over the moisture on his stomach and then work his cock between them, moving seductively over him, back and forth, simulating intercourse.

After several minutes, Blake shudders and then stops me. "The next time I come, I want to be inside you." He slides his hands over my tangled hair. "Let me up, darlin'."

I move onto my back and watch him stride intently into the adjoining bathroom, my gaze fixed on the firm globes of his ass. The water turns on and then off. A minute later, he returns with a towel that he uses to wipe me clean of his semen. He also brings a bottle of some sort that he places on the bedside table along with a strip of condoms.

I eye the bottle, wondering what it is.

He drops the towel onto the floor and gets back in bed, reaching for me.

Even though I'm somewhat embarrassed by my brazen behavior, I want much more of him, so I willingly curl into his embrace. Blake surprises me when he tips up my chin and begins to kiss me with the same intensity and attention to detail he's shown thus far. His tongue is soft but insistent until I open my mouth to let him in. Then he becomes much more forceful, which I love. His hand, rough and coarse from years of hard work, leaves goose bumps in its wake as it moves from my shoulder to my hip.

As his tongue explores the dark recesses of my mouth, his fingers tease the cleft of my ass, tugging lightly on the strip of my thong. The push and pull of my panties has my clit standing up, straining for contact.

I work my leg between his, riding his thigh and seeking relief.

Blake breaks the kiss and buries his face in the curve of my neck. He has my full attention when his finger slides between my ass cheeks to press against my anus. "Has anyone ever taken you here, darlin'?"

I've never been particularly interested in anal sex, nor have my previous lovers, thankfully. Overwhelmed by the idea of doing it with him—and *The Cock*—I shake my head.

"I want to be your first."

I tremble from head to toe at the thought of taking his huge cock there.

Once again reading my thoughts, he says, "I could make it so good for you." His finger teases its way past my resistance, aided by the juices from my pussy, breaching the tight ring of muscle. "So, *so* good."

I gasp at the foreign sensation of being filled there, and moan when he suddenly withdraws. "I need to do this right."

Before I've had a chance to gauge his intentions or ask him what he wants to do right, he's on his knees, tugging my thong off and tossing it over his shoulder. He arranges my legs on either side of him, pushing until they're so far apart, my hips ache from the effort to keep them there.

"That's it." He runs his hands over my inner thighs, teasing the sensitive skin there. "Keep them as far apart as you can." Flopping onto his belly, he drags his tongue over one quivering thigh and then the other. "Hold your lips open," he says, his breath a whisper from my most sensitive flesh. "I need my hands."

Mortified by his request, I feel heat scorch my breasts and face as I comply with his directions. My fingers slide over slippery skin as I hold open my labia for his inspection.

"Gorgeous," he says, blowing a stream of air directly against my clit.

I hold back the urge to scream as he nearly makes me come from that alone.

"Don't hold back. If you want to scream, scream. No one will hear you but me."

God, I'll never be able to look at him again after this night, but at least I'll know what all the hoopla is about, and we haven't even gotten to the main event yet.

He startles me with the first stroke of his tongue.

"Don't let go," he says. "Hold that pretty pussy open for me." The second stroke is no less surprising or stirring as he twirls the tip of his tongue around my clit before encircling it with his lips and tugging lightly. He pushes a finger into my slick channel, curling it up to find a spot no one has ever touched before.

I can't contain the scream as I push against his face and finger.

Adding a second finger, he moves in and out as his tongue and lips focus on my clit. His free hand wraps around my left leg to keep me open wide for him. He continues the dual assault until I'm hit with a second orgasm that's even more powerful than the first.

I'm still coming when he pulls his fingers free of my pussy, leans over me to reach for the bottle on the table, and then pushes a finger into my anus, his entry aided by the cool lubricant he rubbed on his finger. The stroke of his finger sets off another wave of orgasm that makes me see stars. I had no idea I was so sensitive there, and the discovery, on top of all the others, leaves me clinging to what remains of the person I was before I stepped into Blake Dempsey's bedroom.

I come back down to find his tongue lapping up my juices and his finger still buried deep in my ass.

He releases my leg and reaches up to pinch my nipple lightly but insistently. "So, *so* hot, Honey Carmichael. Why'd you wait so long to come to me?" Pushing his finger farther into my ass, he sucks on my clit and sets off a series of small explosions that make my legs quiver and my breath catch. I've never come so much in my life, even with my trusty vibrator.

Right when I'm about to beg him to stop, he suddenly withdraws from me, leaving me a sweating, quivering mess on the bed while he once again retires to the bathroom to clean up.

When he returns, my gaze is drawn to his cock, which stands up tall and proud against his belly, so hard it's purple and slick at the top.

He crawls up on the bed between my legs and settles himself on top of me, holding most of his weight on his elbows. Brushing the hair back off my face, he looks down at me as if taking inventory. "Hi there."

"Hi." I'm still breathing harder than usual and trying to figure out where I should look. If I meet his gaze, I'm afraid I'll give too much away about how completely he's undone me. Remembering Lauren's warning, I'm determined to hold something back. If I give him everything, I'll regret it.

"Look at me."

Trust him not to allow me to hold anything back. I flip my eyes up to make contact with his startlingly blue gaze.

"Are you okay?"

I nod even as I feel the damnable blush flooding my cheeks.

He kisses them both and then my nose and finally my lips. "Ready for the main event?"

I have to look away. "I hope so."

"Are you scared, Honey?"

I bite my lip and nod. "A little."

"I'd never hurt you. You know that, don't you?"

"You used to pinch me," I say, seeking to lighten the moment.

"That was a long time ago." More kisses and the insistent throb of his cock against my belly. "I'd never hurt you now, or do anything you don't want as much as I do."

"Do you want me?"

"So bad." He presses his hips tighter against me. "Can't you feel how bad?"

"Yes." My hands move restlessly on his back, heading to his ass as if drawn by a magnetic pull.

His groan is nearly inhuman. "I can't wait anymore, Honey. I'm going to explode all over you if we don't hurry up." He starts to get up, forcing me to release him. Sitting on the side of the bed, he rolls on a condom.

The XL printed on the wrapper that falls on the bed has me swallowing convulsively.

"Stop thinking. I can hear you thinking."

"I'm not thinking." I'm surprised again by how he seems to get me. No one has ever been able to read me quite so intuitively, and it's unnerving to realize this man I've known all my life might be the only one who can. *Stop. Don't go there. This is one night and one night only. Enjoy every second, but don't get carried away thinking it's something it'll never be.*

Shifting back into position between my legs, he kisses my lips softly and sweetly—so softly and so sweetly, it's hard to remember that I'm not allowed to get carried away.

My hard, throbbing nipples rub against his chest hair as his cock settles into the V of my legs. I can't stop the near-sob that erupts from my chest, belying my bravado.

"Relax, darlin'," he whispers as he kisses my face and neck. "I promise I won't hurt you." He takes himself in hand and runs the tip of his cock from the well of my pussy to my pulsing clit, pausing there to press and retreat several times. The third time he retreats, he pushes the head against my tender opening and thrusts his hips gently.

My first impulse is to tense up.

"Relax."

"Easy for you to say," I say on a grunt. "You're not the one being invaded."

His soft chuckle rumbles through him. "It'll be good, darlin'. Just relax and let me in." He keeps up the steady in and out movements until the head of his cock is lodged firmly inside my pussy. "That's it," he says, resting his forehead on mine and looking down at me. "Feels so good, so tight and hot. Does it feel good to you, too?"

Even though I'm stretched almost to the point of discomfort, it doesn't hurt. The sense of fullness is amazing as he awakens every nerve ending on his way inside me. "Yes, it feels good." I squirm under him, seeking something—whether it's relief or further penetration, I can't say.

"Ready for some more?" he asks several minutes later.

"I think so."

He rocks in and out in small strokes, my slickness guiding his entry. And then he pushes harder, sinking in farther than he's been yet. Reaching for my left leg, he hooks his arm under my knee and pushes it back to my chest, opening me wider.

I'm consumed by him, pinned to the bed by the thick length of his cock inside me as he rocks and strokes his way deeper.

Sweat beads on his brow and pools between us as he moves back and forth, pushing and pulling in a rhythm that sets my entire body on fire.

"Okay?" he asks after many minutes of strained silence as we work together in silent accord.

"Yes! *Yes*." My fingers dig into his ass as I pull him to me, wanting to keep him still for a minute while I throb and stretch around him. I can't imagine how he thinks I'll ever take him in my ass when he's got my pussy stretched to its absolute limit. Pushing that worrisome thought to the back of my mind, I focus on the burning, throbbing sensations coming from my core.

"Just a little more," he whispers through gritted teeth, clearly clinging to his control.

I release an unsteady laugh. "*More?*"

"The wide part," he says with a teasing grin.

"Christ have mercy."

That makes him laugh as he pushes my leg tighter against my chest. "Put your other leg around my hip."

My muscles quiver as if they're made of jelly, but I somehow manage to do what he asks.

"There," he says, releasing a sigh of relief. "That's good." With another mighty shove, he's fully seated with his balls brushing against my ass. For a long time, he stays right there, all the way inside, throbbing and pulsing against me as my internal muscles clutch and contract around him. "Want to go for a ride, darlin'?" he asks in a low, sexy tone that makes my nipples tingle.

Before I can form a reply, he begins to move, slowly at first and then with more purpose, encouraged by my moans of pleasure and the moisture that pours forth from me, easing the way. The slow climb begins again, each stroke building on the one before until I stand at the brink of something so big and so powerful, my impulse is to hide from it. Somehow I know that this one will change me forever, and I fight it with every ounce of fortitude I can muster during the most astonishing sex of my life.

He seems to sense the battle I'm waging with myself and takes the decision out of my hands when he reaches down to where we're joined, presses his fingers to my clit and sends me into orbit.

Groaning loudly, he goes with me, pushing so hard into me, I feel the heat of his release deep inside even as I crest the waves of my own wild ride. I've never imagined anything like the power we've created together.

His arms give out, and he collapses on top of me, not crushing me but surrounding me with his scent and his heat as he continues to throb inside me. Against my skin, I can feel the hard beat of his heart and hear his panting breath.

I need to get out of here. I have to collect what's left of my senses and go home.

CHAPTER THREE

Honey

Blake speaks first. "That was... I don't have the words."

All I can think about is escaping while I still can. "I need to get up."

"Oh, sorry. Didn't mean to trap you under me." His withdrawal isn't much easier than his entry, and I wince as tender tissues ripple and stretch around him. With one hand around the end of the condom to hold it in place, he finally pulls free of me.

By then, I'm breathing heavily and perspiring again. On less than steady legs, I go to the bathroom, trying not to imagine how I must look from behind. My hair is a tangled mess, and the sight that greets me in the mirror is nothing short of frightening. I look like a woman who's been well and truly ravished.

"Well, you got exactly what you wanted," I whisper to my reflection. On the vanity, I find a brush and drag it through my hair. I splash water on my flaming cheeks and blot my face dry with a hand towel that smells like him. My nipples have gone from their usual pink shade to bright red thanks to his attention.

"Oh God," I say out loud as a tremble shakes my body. "*God.*" With my hands on the counter, I let my head hang low, rolling it back and forth to relieve the tension in my shoulders.

This was a huge mistake—a mistake of epic proportions. In one hour, he's managed to ruin me for all other men. Every other guy will be measured against him and found lacking, in more ways than one. The one thing I know for sure is I need to get the hell out of here before I make things worse than they already are.

His warm hands landing on my shoulders startle me out of my musings and mess with my resolve to escape. Pressing his fingers into muscles gone hard with tension, he kneads and strokes until they yield to him. Even my muscles are taking his side.

"I need to go," I say, even though I'm not sure I can still walk.

"Why?" As his talented fingers continue their work, his lips find my neck, stirring a body so recently and thoroughly satisfied back to life.

I wriggle free of him and duck into the separate room that houses the toilet. I take care of business and rest my head against the cool wood door for a long moment, working up the wherewithal to leave. Lauren's warning rings through my mind like church bells on Sunday. *It's only sex. You won't find a home with him.*

When I feel ready to face him and say what needs to be said, I open the door to find him leaning against the vanity in all his naked glory. Arms crossed over his broad chest, he watches me with the same intense scrutiny I've come to expect from him.

At some point, he disposed of the condom and his cock has hardened again. I wonder if he's always hard.

"No," he says. "It's you."

"How do you do that?"

"Do what?"

"Know exactly what I'm thinking."

"Because your every thought and emotion shows on your face. You'd be a terrible poker player, darlin'."

"Is that so?" I cross my arms over my breasts and stare at him. "What am I thinking now?"

"You're wondering how you can thank me for the lay and get the hell out of here without hurting my feelings."

My mouth falls open, but I force it closed and continue to stare at him. *How* does he do that?

As if he has not a care in the world, he strolls across the spacious bathroom until he's close enough for me to breathe in the bewitching scent of soap and sex he brings with him. "I don't want you to go."

"I have to."

"No, you don't." His hands land on my hips, drawing me into his magical web once again. "We're just getting started."

I shake my head. "I can't do this. I thought I could, but I can't."

"What can't you do, Honey bee?" He loops his arms around me, bringing all our most important parts back into contact.

"For one thing, I can't talk to you when you're touching me this way."

His face lifts into a half grin that is utterly charming—and disarming. Releasing me but keeping his hands on my hips, he says, "Is that better?"

"A little."

"Talk to me. Tell me what's wrong. Did I hurt you? I tried so hard not to."

"No, of course not. You didn't hurt me."

"Then what is it?"

I take a moment to gather my thoughts. "I thought I could have sex with you and not want it to be anything more, but if I stay, if we do... *that*... again..."

"Ah, I see," he says, affecting a grave expression that reminds me of how he looked after the awful accident during our senior year of high school. Back then, I wanted so badly to offer comfort he never would've accepted from me—or anyone. "You might want to stay longer, and knowing my reputation, that wouldn't be wise."

"Yes." I'm relieved that he seems to understand. Have I ever had a more serious conversation in which both parties are stark naked? Not that I can recall.

"Can I let you in on a little secret?"

I'd expected him to send me on my way, grateful that I hadn't done what scores of others before me had probably tried and failed to do—change him. "Um, sure."

"Remember a month or so ago when I saw you at Matt and Julie's party?"

I nod. "I remember."

"And do you remember what you said to me in the bar tonight?"

I let my forehead drop to his chest. "I'm trying to forget."

His soft laugh makes his chest rumble. "I wanted to say the same thing to you that night at Matt's house. I can still remember exactly what you were wearing—a dress that had flowers on it and was all frilly and girly, and it showed off the tops of the spectacular breasts that've inspired many of my wet dreams over the years." As he speaks, he drags his index fingers over the tops of my breasts. "And sky-high heels that showed off your endless legs. I had a hard-on all night with your name on it."

I look up at him. "Do you mean that? You thought of me that way? Before tonight?"

"Honey Carmichael, I've thought of you that way since we were in second grade. Why do you think I was always pinching you?"

"I *knew* you remembered!"

Chuckling, he says, "You've always been hard to forget. And you'll be especially hard to forget now that I know how soft your skin is and that your Gran nicknamed you well, because you taste like honey all over."

"So what're you saying?"

"I want you to stay awhile longer."

"What does 'awhile' mean?"

"For me, it means spending the night. I'm not capable of forever or love or white dresses or picket fences. That'll never be me." His expression darkens considerably.

"Because of Jordan."

"For one thing."

"That was such a long time ago, Blake. I don't want you to think I'm advocating on my own behalf, because I have no illusions that I might be the one to change your mind. But I knew her, and I loved her, and I can't believe she'd expect you to spend the rest of your life alone because of an accident."

"I'd rather not talk about her, if that's okay."

"I understand. It's still painful."

"Always will be."

"So then you're proposing an all-nighter?" I ask with a coy grin, hoping to make him smile again.

His lips twist into a half smile. "If you can handle it. Are you up for that?"

"I could be."

"Before you decide for sure, you should know I have a condition."

"What kind of condition?"

"When we're in bed, I'm in charge."

Although his words are wildly arousing, I can't roll over and play dead on this one. "So I don't get to please you?"

"Pleasing you pleases me."

Well, damn... "What I did to you before..."

"Was spectacular, and I'll definitely want more."

"Okay, good, because it was spectacular for me, too."

His eyes go dark with lust, and his cock bumps up against my belly, letting me know it approves. "Any objections?"

I shake my head. There's a certain sort of comfort and safety that comes from having known him all my life. "So what happens now?"

"We go back to bed. I'm not finished with you yet."

I glance down at The Cock, which is standing tall and proud, looking up at me. "I don't know if I can take him again. I'm a little sore from the first time."

He takes my hand and begins to walk backward to his bedroom. "There's lots of other stuff we can do."

"Like what?"

Blake cups my cheeks. "I'd love to get to know this fine ass a little better, for one thing."

I gulp at the thought of that monstrous cock breaching me there. He'd rip me apart.

"No, I wouldn't."

I pull my hand free of his grip. "Stop doing that!"

"What am I doing?"

"Reading my mind!"

"I already told you. It's not my fault that every thought you have is reflected in your expression."

"How is it reflected in my expression? How did you read 'I'm afraid he'll rip me apart'?"

His face twists into a grimace that indeed conveys that exact thought. "And FYI, I will not rip you apart. I like you put together exactly the way you are." With his hands once again caressing my ass, he speaks softly against my ear, sending goose bumps cascading down my back and arms. "I'd prepare you so well, you wouldn't even know I was there."

The utter preposterousness of that comment has me snorting with laughter. "Right... And how would you prepare me to take that *thing* and walk away intact?"

"Ouch. That *thing* is insulted." He strokes his cock soothingly, as if tending to its feelings.

"I'm sure he'll get over it the next time I spread my legs."

"He's already over it knowing there'll be a next time."

I laugh. "You're outrageous."

Smiling, he says, "Lie down and get comfortable."

With one eye over my shoulder in an attempt to gauge his intentions, I do as directed.

"Face down."

Filled with trepidation about where this might be leading, I turn over, hugging a pillow to my chest.

Blake goes into the bathroom and returns holding something that I can't see because he's adjusted the dimmer switch until the room is nearly dark.

Every inch of my body tingles with awareness of him as he settles on the bed next to me. Between my legs, desire thrums like a heartbeat, pulsing and twitching for more even after what I've already had.

"Relax, Honey," he says softly, his hand moving over my back, aided by something slick and fragrant. "Close your eyes and relax. Let me take care of you."

Massage oil. That's what I smelled, and good Lord, he has magical hands to go along with his magical dick. I moan from the pleasure of him kneading the tension from my muscles. He works from my shoulders to my ribs to my waist, skipping my bottom and taking care of each leg, moving with leisurely strokes that make my pussy throb and drip.

I squirm on the bed, trying to find relief.

"Don't move."

"But—"

"Don't. Move." He leans over me, speaking directly into my ear. "I'm in charge here. Remember?"

Letting out a deep breath filled with frustration and need, I try to do as I'm told, but I can't help squiggling a little bit as he kneads my inner thighs. A sharp, stinging slap to my ass has me crying out in surprise.

"I told you not to move."

"Did you... You didn't just..."

"Yes, I did, and I'll do it again if you can't behave." As he speaks, he caresses the heated area on my bottom, which only makes the throb between my legs sharper. Leaning over me again, he says, "Have you ever been spanked, Honey?"

"N-no."

"Oh damn. I get to be your first?"

Before I know what's happening, he has me over his lap, my bottom in the air as he rubs the oil deep into my cheeks, running his finger down the crease that separates them.

Though I'm outraged at the thought of him spanking me, I'm so turned on, I can't find the words to express that outrage.

"This isn't about punishment, baby." He continues to caress and stroke and tease my most sensitive flesh. "This is about desire."

All this time... Blake Dempsey has been right here, able to unleash a side of me I'd never known existed, the side that wants him to do all the things he mentioned and everything else he can think of. I want it all.

"What're you thinking right now?"

"You tell me. You're an expert at reading my mind."

"I can't see your face, so I don't know. That's why I'm asking. Tell me."

I clear my throat and try to find the words. My Gran raised me to be a lady, and a lady doesn't say the things I'm thinking to a man. I try not to think about what she'd have to say about what I said to him in the bar. "I can't believe you were here all this time and I didn't know..."

"What didn't you know?" His voice is rough and gruff, and his cock presses against my belly, hard and insistent.

"That you were like this."

"What am I like?"

"Passionate." I lick lips that have gone dry while I waited to see what he would do next. "Adventuresome. Dirty."

That last one has him laughing. "I'm dirtier than you can imagine. You think you can match me dirty for dirty, Honey Carmichael?"

"I think I want to try."

"Fuck, that's a good answer." To reward me, he spanks my other cheek, sending a tingle of heat and need straight to my clit. Before I can recover, he spanks the other side, rotating back and forth until I'm a drooling, blathering mess of nerves and heat and sensation—and on the verge of coming again.

He follows each spank with a caress that sets me on fire. I had no idea whatsoever that my bottom is such an erogenous zone. His hands never stop moving, top to bottom, lifting, separating, dipping into the crease and pressing against my anus but never breaching me.

I can barely keep up with the barrage of sensations overtaking me as he leaves no part of my ass untouched. And then... I'm moving and landing face down again on the bed and, oh my God... Is that his tongue? On my... Oh *God*. Oh... He's licking me *there*, circling my back entrance with insistent stabs of his tongue, and nothing in my life has ever felt quite like that—dark and forbidden and incredible.

"Don't come," he says as he holds my cheeks apart for his tongue. "No matter what I do, do *not* come."

I try to reply. I really do, but my brain cells are completely fried.

"Honey. Do you hear me?"

"*Yes*," I say on a sob.

"Up on your knees." He pulls at my waist, positioning me where he wants me, until I'm bent at the waist, my ass in the air and my weight supported by my elbows and knees. With my legs quivering madly, I feel like a wanton, brazen slut, but I can't seem to care that I'm all but jamming my ass into Blake Dempsey's face.

Oh dear God... Gran, if you're watching over me like you said you always would, please take the rest of the night off. Please...

CHAPTER FOUR

Honey

I drag myself to work at noon on Saturday, and only because a family from Dallas has driven hours to Marfa for one of my Desert Babies custom photo shoots. What began as a lark has turned into a booming business, and I couldn't be more thrilled to see my photo studio's following growing so rapidly. Most of the time, I'm excited about my work. Today, I'm too sore and stunned and sleep-deprived and... I'm a hot mess, for lack of a better term.

In one long unforgettable night, Blake Dempsey has ruined my life. I'll never have sex like that with anyone else. I know this because I've been with enough guys to attest that no one does it like him—and none of them can begin to compete with The Cock. Lauren was right about that.

I can't believe I took that thing a second and then a *third* time, which is why I can barely move today without every tender part of me screaming in protest. The pain reminds me of when Gran signed me up for riding lessons, and I couldn't sit down for a week after the first lesson. In time, I got used to the saddle, but if I had fifty years with Blake, I don't think my body would ever become accustomed to or comfortable with that cock.

Hours after I crawled from his bed, a shell of the woman I'd been when I arrived, I can still feel him inside me. My muscles are still contracting. My clit is still pulsating with aftershocks on top of aftershocks. Surely this can't be *normal*. Maybe I ought to call my doctor. Except what would I tell him? Blake Dempsey and his giant cock fucked me to within an inch of my life, and I'm concerned that I might've sustained internal injuries?

I can't imagine saying those words to the lovely old doctor I've been going to all my life. He'd die of shock.

Before I unlock the studio for today's shoot, I stop into the café next door for a tall cup of coffee and one of my friend Scarlett's melt-in-your-mouth scones. In addition to aching from stem to stern, I'm also famished. Blake was right—burning all those calories between the sheets requires a lot of fuel.

"Morning, Honey." Scarlett is always so damned chipper. I think it's probably because she consumes coffee all day. That has to be it. She's about my age, with a flawless complexion and long dark hair that she wears in one braid down her back when she's working. "Or is it afternoon now?"

"Just about," I mutter.

"You all right?" Scarlett leans in for a closer look, which has me taking a step back. "Is that..." Lowering her voice, she says, "Razor burn? Honey! I thought you'd sworn off contact with species who have to shave their faces every day."

"I have. I did."

Scarlett raises her brows, her dark eyes gone wide with shock. "Has someone fallen off the wagon? Your lips are swollen, too." Leaning her elbows on the counter, she settles in for a good long gossip session. "Anything else swollen?"

Everything is swollen, not that I plan to tell Scarlett that. "Gotta go. Got a shoot in ten."

"I want the dirty details!" she calls after me.

"Not happening," I say to myself as well as the older man who holds the door for me.

"Pardon?" he says.

"Nothing." I blame Blake for this. He's not only got me talking to myself but to strangers, too. At the next storefront over from Scarlett's place, I unlock the front door of my studio and switch the sign from Closed to Open. With each step I take toward my office in the back of the studio, every muscle in my body protests the Olympic sex-a-thon I participated in last night.

I'm still trying to process what happened in Blake's bed, and it's been two hours since I dragged myself from his warm embrace, got dressed and managed to get my car out of his garage without waking him. Or if I woke him, he didn't come out to see me off, which is just as well. I'm not sure I'm ready to face him. Hell, I won't be ready to face him a year from now after the things we did.

When he said "all night," he wasn't kidding. He finally took mercy on me around four thirty in the morning when I cried uncle after my seventh—or was it the eighth?—orgasm. I think it might've been eight. His reputation as a sex machine is well earned, that's for sure.

I take a seat at my desk and wince from the ache that spreads from between my legs to my thighs and even my poor bum. He never did make good on his "threat" to take me there, but I know he wanted to. If we were to get together again, I have a feeling that might be on the menu, although I still can't imagine how he'd ever...

Dropping my head into my hands, I can't believe that I'm tingling with arousal at the very thought of something I've never even considered before last night. If he's got me thinking about *that*—and actually *wanting* it—his sexual gifts extend far beyond his incredible "endowment."

The bells ring on the front door, and I bite back a groan, hoping my clients aren't early, because I'm nowhere near ready for them.

"Honey, where are you?" Lauren calls out, her voice echoing in the vast space that is my studio.

"Back here." I should've known it would be her, coming to get the scoop along with the dirty details.

She comes breezing in, wearing an adorable tank dress that shows off her amazing biceps. My bestie is a gym rat of the highest order and could kick ass on most of the men we know, which she says is why she never gets asked out anymore. Not that that stops her from lifting just about every day. I'm envious of those biceps but not the discipline it takes to get them. Maybe if I were in better shape, I wouldn't feel like I was ridden hard and put up wet last night. And this morning.

Looking absolutely gorgeous with her curly blonde hair in a messy bun and big brown eyes fully made up, she comes to the doorway of the office to take a good long look at me. "*Well*..." Rolling her hand, she begs for details.

"You were right. He's all that *and* a bag of chips."

"He's all that and *ten* bags of chips."

"Agreed."

"So you had the big O?"

"I think I had eight big Os. I lost count."

"Shut the front door! *Eight?* Holy shit, Honey!"

"I'm so sore, I can't move, and I'm shooting twins today." I groan at the thought of the workout awaiting me. My job is very physical when I'm shooting one baby. Two will about kill me today.

Lauren snickers. "So The Cock lived up to its reputation."

"The Cock is a battering ram. My poor va-jay-jay will never be the same."

"I remember that. The day after the first time was like losing my V card all over again. Hurt like hell. But after a while, I suppose you get used to *it*."

"I can't imagine ever getting used to *that*."

"Well, Blake being Blake, you probably won't get the chance to get used to it. He's becoming more remote all the time. I worry about him —as a friend," she quickly adds. "Did he say anything about getting together again?"

"Not really," I say, recalling the conversation in his bedroom when he convinced me to spend the night.

Lauren sighs loudly. "I have a confession to make..."

"What?"

"When I encouraged you to proposition him, I was hoping to kill two birds with one stone."

"How so?"

"I wanted you to finally get properly and thoroughly laid, and I was sort of hoping you might be just what he needs, someone he's known forever who he can trust to let go a little with."

"Yeah, well, he let go all right, but it was all sex and nothing more than a few moments of nostalgia about the playground years."

"What about the playground?"

"He used to pinch me and make me cry, which he pretended to not remember, but of course he totally did. He said he pinched me because he liked me. Boys are so weird, and they grow up to be even weirder men."

"He's one of the good ones." Lauren's expression is sadder than I've seen it since my Gran died. "Losing Jordan messed him up permanently. It's like he's broken on the inside or something. It's such a waste of a good man. He'd be a wonderful husband and father if only he could find a way to forgive himself for something that wasn't even his fault."

"It is sad," I agree. "He's a good guy who deserves better than the hand he was dealt by fate."

"You didn't... You know... Start to think..."

"No! I told you I wouldn't, and I didn't. It was just sex. I know that. He knows that. One and done."

"Oh good. Phew. I was worried all night that you'd get so wrapped up in The Cock's magic spell that you'd forget."

"The Cock's magic spell." I sputter with laughter at her terminology.

"Is it or is it not a magical cock?"

"It's quite magical in the moment. The day after?" I switch positions and nearly gasp from the shock of almost painful arousal that refuses to quit, even hours after I left his house. "Not so magical."

"A hot bath with Epsom salts. That's what you need."

I nearly moan at the thought of my tortured lower half soaking in hot water, knowing I'm hours away from being able to do it.

"I'll drop some stuff off on your porch on my way home. It'll fix you right up."

"You're the best friend ever, but I blame you for my current predicament."

"Your pre-*dick*-ament. Ha-ha. You loved every second of it. Admit it."

"I really did."

"I knew it!"

"It was like a light went on or something. I finally get why everyone else goes nuts over it."

"Praise the Lord. She's seen the light."

"Yes, I have."

"So why do you seem so bummed? I thought you'd be all euphoric and glowy today, but you're not."

"Glowy?"

"After eight orgasms, there ought to be a bit of a glow to you."

"I'm not bummed. I'm..." I can lie to some people. Lauren isn't one of them. "Okay, maybe I'm a little bummed."

"Why?"

"Don't get mad at me when I say I'm sad that all it can ever be is what happened last night. I knew that going in. You warned me. I warned myself. He even warned me. But that doesn't stop me from wishing things were different, that *he* was different."

She blanches. "Honey, you *promised* me!"

I hold up a hand to stop her from going off. "I know I did, and I still know the score. I only wish it didn't have to be this way. That's all. He's so..."

"Perfect in every way except for the hole in his chest where his heart used to be?"

I sputter with laughter at her spot-on description, but just as quickly, my laughter turns to tears because it's so true. I bitterly resent the tears.

"Oh, Honey." She gets up and comes around the desk to hug me. "I told you not to do this. I *told* you!"

"I'm not doing it. I'm having a teeny, tiny pity party that will last an hour and a half max, and then I'm moving on. I swear."

"All right." She sighs again as she pats my hair like the mother hen she is where I'm concerned. As a girl whose mother left her at a church to be raised by strangers, I drink in all the mothering I can get. "I suppose I can allow that after what you experienced last night."

She stays for a little while, long enough for me to mostly get myself together before my clients show up with a clatter and a bang and the ringing of the bells on the door. Why do they always make so much noise when they arrive?

"Showtime," Lauren whispers. "Are you okay?"

"I will be. Losing myself in work for a few hours will help." I call out to let the clients know I'll be right with them.

"I'll see you at Julie's party tonight, right?"

"*What?* That's *tonight?*"

"Yes, you dummy," she says, laughing. "You knew this. We talked about going in on a gift for her two days ago, before you had your brain pickled by The Cock."

"Oh my God! He's friends with Matt! He'll be there! I can't see him! It's too soon."

"You have to go, Honey. Julie is one of your best friends, and Blake will be a perfect gentleman. You know he will."

This conversation is being conducted in loud whispers so my clients won't overhear us.

"How will I ever look at him again and not think about that *weapon* he has in his pants?"

Lauren is laughing so hard, tears fill her eyes. "The same way the rest of us who've experienced the weapon do—we don't look down. No matter what, *don't look down.*"

"Don't look down. I can do that." I tell her what she wants to hear, but honestly, I'm wondering how I'll look anywhere but *down* when I see him again. That party is going to be pure torture.

Blake

I wake up alone and feel oddly disappointed that she's gone. Disappointment isn't something I normally feel after a night with a hot woman, but Honey isn't just any hot woman. She's a friend, too, and our shared history makes her different. That's exactly why I usually stay away from sleeping with women I grew up with in Marfa. I know them too well, but when a woman like Honey walks into a bar and asks me to fuck her, well, I'm only human, and she's a freaking goddess.

I've always thought so, even in high school when I was in love with Jordan and planning to spend my life with her. Honey was the untouchable queen of all things Marfa High School—homecoming queen, prom queen, cheerleading captain. In other words, off-limits to mere mortals. And that was fine with me. From tenth grade on, I was completely enthralled by Jordan and didn't give a thought to being with any other girl the way I was with her.

We were going to get married right after high school and have four babies—every two years for eight years. And then, when they were grown, we would travel and see the world. All our plans were shattered the afternoon a semi ran a stop sign, killing her instantly and injuring me so badly, I spent a month in ICU. For a time, the doctors told my parents to prepare for the worst.

I survived, but I've never been the same. I miss Jordan every day and have never stopped thinking about what might've been for us. I have no memory of the crash itself, but I have vivid nightmares in which my brain imagines what it must've been like, forcing me to relive the horror over and over again. That's one reason why I rarely spend the night with a woman. Do I need the whole town talking about Blake Dempsey's pathetic night terrors?

That wouldn't be good for business, the one area of my life that's actually satisfying and successful, and I intend to keep it that way.

It's weird to feel disappointed about waking up alone when I wake up alone every day of my life and wouldn't have it any other way. Like Honey said, I never bring women home with me anymore. It's too messy when I want them to leave and can't think of any other way to get them out but to ask them to go. They're all the same. They all hope they're going to be the one to fix Blake Dempsey's broken heart.

What they don't know is my heart shattered the day Jordan was killed, and it doesn't exist anymore as anything other than an organ that pumps blood. It doesn't *feel* anything. It took three years after Jordan died for me to have sex with someone else, and that was a total cluster fuck. I broke down into pathetic sobs that scared the hell out of the poor girl I'd chosen to get me back on the horse.

Thank goodness that happened during my brief stint at UT Austin, far enough away from Marfa that no one who mattered ever heard about it. A year after that, I got totally wasted with a girl in a bar and did it again, this time without the histrionics. I declared myself cured and got back on the horse in a big way with a different woman any time I wanted one, all of them knowing the score before they went to bed with me—one night and one night only.

My system-wide numbness makes for a drama-free, peaceful existence most of the time. I mean, it's not every day that a woman like Honey propositions me in a bar, and she more than lived up to the nickname her Gran gave her by calling her "Honey" for her entire childhood. Her real name is Evelyn, but no one has ever called her anything other than Honey.

Now I know she tastes like the sweetest honey I've ever had, and hours after I last touched her, I can still taste her on my lips and smell her scent in my bed. Am I really lying here on a rare free Saturday thinking about a woman? Yeah, I guess I am, probably because I'm surprised that a guy as jaded as I am can still have his world rocked once in a while.

She rocked me by walking into a bar so far below her usual hangout, it's not even in her stratosphere. She rocked—and shocked—me with what she said. And then she totally rocked me with how she responded to me. It's no secret that Honey Carmichael has dated her way through many of the single guys under forty in Marfa, so it was interesting to discover how innocent she really is underneath her smooth, sophisticated veneer.

I never would've guessed, for example, that she's never been spanked or had her ass played with or come as hard as she did many times last night. Just thinking about the squeeze of her pussy around my cock makes me hard. She was so small and tight, and it was such a battle to enter her—a battle I loved all three times I coaxed her into trying.

Wrapping my hand around my cock, I stroke from base to tip, nice and slow as I relive the night with Honey, from the second she uttered those unforgettable words in the bar to the third time I came inside her. I wonder if she's sore today, if she's thinking about me the way I'm thinking about her, if she'd want do it again if she were still here…

I close my eyes, remembering the way her big, round breasts heaved with every deep thrust of my cock. God, I loved watching them move and the way her nipples dragged against my chest. I'm starting to feel the telltale tingle at the base of my spine, and I'm dripping pre-cum onto my hand, but that makes the up-and-down slide easier and hotter.

I don't want to come yet, so I slow it down and recall her shock when I fingered her ass. No one had ever touched her there, and I take a perverse thrill in knowing I was the first. I let my mind wander to what it'd be like to fuck her there, how she'd writhe and grunt and scream when I forced my way past the tight ring of muscle that would try to keep me out.

I'd have us both so slick with lube that I'd be able to push into her until my balls are tucked up against her pussy and she's taken the widest part of my cock. I'd keep her coming the whole time so she'd be in a hot frenzy, unable to do anything other than take me over and over and over again until I come deep inside the most private part of her.

I picture her ass stretching to accommodate me, and that's all it takes to send me over the edge, the hot splash of my release covering my abdomen and flooding my hand. I'm gasping from how hard I came, almost as hard as I did with her during the night.

It was good with her, I concede as my heart rate and breathing slow to normal. The best sex I've had since Jordan died, if I'm being honest with myself. It was comforting being with someone I've known all my life, someone who knew me before I lost Jordan and who still cares about me, even though I've given her no reason to.

And then it occurs to me that tonight is the surprise party for Julie's thirtieth birthday. Julie is one of Honey's lifelong friends, and Matt is one of mine. As I get out of bed and head for the shower, I try to pretend that my lifeless heart didn't give a happy little jolt at knowing I'll get to see her again later.

I can't wait.

CHAPTER FIVE

Honey

The shoot is a disaster from the get-go, with two cranky babies and parents who try to micromanage every aspect. I want to tell the parents to come back in an hour, but I can't do that, so I put up with them, nodding in the right places while doing it my way in the end. My way is what people come from all over for.

Before I had the idea for my Desert Babies series, my studio was on the verge of bankruptcy. People don't hire photographers the way they did before the digital age brought do-it-yourself photography into vogue. Weddings were the backbone of my business until the bridal magazines started touting candid photos taken by guests as an alternative to one of the biggest expenses—the photographer. Don't even get me started on what cameras built into smartphones did to my already struggling business.

I'd begun to panic about how I'd survive if the studio went under when I stumbled upon the idea for the Desert Babies, quite by accident, late one night when flipping through a magazine that featured

Anne Geddes's distinctive baby photos. Then I moved on to a local magazine that had photos of the desert outside Marfa, the rolling hills of West Texas and the wild vegetation. The two things had come together to give me the idea that I began implementing the next day by designing props and costumes and backdrops that plopped the babies into the environment in clever and inviting ways.

After I posted the first shots to my Facebook page, the idea was an immediate hit, with word-of-mouth publicity bringing in clients from all over the state. It surpassed my wildest dreams, and I have a waiting list a month out. However, the success of my idea means I spend a lot of time with babies who are often less than accommodating of my vision and that of their harried parents.

Today is one of the worst shoots I've had since I started the program a year ago. The mom is a total pain in the ass with her endless demands. The dad is a useless doormat who does whatever she tells him to do, and the babies... Well, I hate to say this about innocent children, but they aren't photogenic. It happens sometimes, and I'm usually able to make lemonade from lemons. I do what I can with these two and have my "money" shots in the first hour, not that the mom will hear that. She forces us through two more interminable hours, after which her twins are in full-on meltdown mode, and I'm wishing I kept vodka on hand in the studio.

By the time they finally leave, I'm feeling almost as sorry for the kids who have to grow up with her as I feel for myself, having lost three hours I'll never get back dealing with her. My body hurts so badly I can barely walk as I leave the studio two hours before Julie's surprise party and head home to the house my Gran left me when she died.

I adore the thirties-era Craftsman that Gran lovingly restored over the years, one room at a time, until every inch of the two-thousand-square-foot home gleamed with new floors, paint and windows, some of which are stained-glass beauties she found at antique stores and yard sales.

She went with desert landscaping outside so we wouldn't have to mow grass in the heat of the summer. Cactus and gravel require very little upkeep. Gran was right about that, but then again, she was right about most things. It took me four years after she died to move into the larger master bedroom suite that I will always think of as hers, but she disliked nothing more than pointless sentiment, and she would've protested me being squashed into my tiny bedroom when her much larger one was going unused.

Lauren helped me make the room my own and mopped up my tears when I finally got around to packing up Gran's things and donating her clothing to the needy, which she would've loved. She was forever giving away money she didn't have to help people who were less fortunate than she was, not to mention taking in a baby abandoned at the church and raising her as her own.

I kept her good jewelry along with photographs of her parents, siblings and cousins, all of whom predeceased her. They were the closest thing to family that I've ever had, even if I never met any of them. I count those photographs and the ones I have of her among my most prized possessions.

I limp onto the porch, where I find that Lauren has come through with a basket of Epsom salts and other bath products. I moan with anticipation of sinking into Gran's cast-iron, claw-foot tub. Because this day has been a total bitch, I fix myself a tall glass of wine and a plate of crackers, cheese and grapes to tide me over until the party.

In the bathroom, I set my drink and snack on the windowsill, light a few candles and sprinkle the new bath beads and salts Lauren got me into the steaming water. Before I turn off the lights, I kick off my cowboy boots and strip out of my dress and underwear. I catch a glimpse of my ass in the mirror and gasp at the fingertip bruises that stand out in stark contrast to my white flesh. Turning to face the mirror, I see that there are also bruises on my hips and breasts, and I shiver, remembering the way he touched me with such all-consuming hunger. Thank goodness he didn't leave bruises anywhere people could see them.

My nipples tighten and my clit springs to life, making me groan as I wonder how it's possible I have any gas left in my tank after last night. Sinking into the hot water is almost as orgasmic an experience as fucking Blake Dempsey was. If my poor, tortured flesh could actually sigh with pleasure, it'd be hyperventilating at how good the hot water and Epsom salts feel.

I lay back against the pillow I bought just for the tub and reach for my glass of wine. During the shoot, I forced my mind to stay on the subject at hand, hoping I'd get rid of them sooner rather than later. We all know how that worked out. So it's been a few hours since I did a full review of last night's activities, and I let my mind wander back to the bar, to the way he choked on his beer after I delivered my opening line, to how he whispered gruffly in my ear to follow him home, how he insisted on feeding me before we got down to it, and the way he completely obliterated my memories of all other men in one incredible night.

How did he manage that last part? Well, The Cock managed it. That thought makes me laugh. I have to admit I thought Lauren was exaggerating when she said she's never seen one quite like Blake's. Now I know she wasn't exaggerating. If anything, her descriptions didn't do The Cock justice. Just thinking about it makes me tingle all over. He made me feel like a newly deflowered virgin trying to take him into my protesting body. The struggle was epic and my reactions unprecedented. I've never come from penetration alone. It usually takes a lot more than that, but not with Blake. Not with The Cock that stroked every nerve ending I possess into an unholy orgasmic frenzy.

Picking it all apart with the perspective I lacked in the moment, I realize it was more than his equipment that set me on fire. It was the way he paid such close attention to my every reaction, the way he touched me and stroked me and sucked on my nipples with my ultimate pleasure as his only goal.

I return my wineglass to the windowsill and fill my hands with my breasts, running my thumbs gently over sore nipples that immediately respond by getting even harder. I draw in a sharp deep breath at the connection between my nipples and clit. I'm amazed that thinking about last night has me fully aroused once again.

My legs move restlessly, sending water sloshing toward the sides of the tall tub.

Closing my eyes, I relive it, from those first minutes in the bar to sneaking out this morning and everything in between. As if it's happening all over again, I can almost feel the press of his huge cock against my opening, stretching me to my absolute limit as he works his way inside.

I bite my lip and send a hand down to tend to my tingling clit. Oh, that feels good, even if I'm still so sore and tender. I take it easy as I rub slow, soft circles around the tight knot of nerves while continuing to tweak my nipple. It usually takes much more than this to get myself off, but remembering the things he did, the places he touched me with his fingers, tongue and cock, has me on the verge of exploding in no time at all.

Was I really bent over in half on his bed, my ass in the air while he tongued me *there*? Thinking about what we must've looked like in that position, I inhale a shuddering breath as the memories of how it felt and how much I loved it send me careening into an intense orgasm. Water spills over the sides of the tub, but I can't bring myself to care as it goes on and on, as if I haven't come more in the last twenty-four hours than I have at any one time ever.

Afterward, I slide deeper into the water, completely relaxed and depleted. I could go to bed now and sleep until tomorrow morning, but I can't do that. I can't disappoint Julie, who would be crushed if I missed her thirtieth birthday party. With my own three-oh right around the corner, I can't do that to her. Besides, Blake will be there, and I'm on fire with curiosity about whether it'll be different between us after last night.

Though I know I shouldn't be excited to see him again, that's what gets me out of the tub twenty minutes later. It's what has me spending extra time on my hair and makeup and dressing with careful thought in the same frilly, feminine dress he liked so much the last time we were at Matt and Julie's. Because I'm a Texas girl through and through, I put on my red cowboy boots to complete the outfit and grab a denim jacket in case Matt has the AC on the frost setting, as usual.

I look good. I feel better than I did before the bath. I feel ready to see him again.

———

I wasn't ready to see him again. I feel like I'm wearing a neon sign on my head that says *Blake fucked my lights out last night.* I'm sure everyone must know, when no one does, except Lauren, and she wouldn't tell anyone. Well, Blake knows, too, and more than once, I feel his intense blue eyes trained on me as if he's seeing me naked right there in the midst of our friends.

I never should've propositioned him the way I did, but I can't seem to regret the stupendous sex I had with him. If only I didn't actually have to *see* him today, but I'd forgotten about Julie's birthday when I decided last night was the night after weeks of trying to work up the nerve to put Lauren's plan into motion.

Thus one of the three times a year I run into Blake had to happen the day after we had the wildest, dirtiest sex of my life. Judging from the smug, satisfied expression on his face, he knows I'm uncomfortable, and he's enjoying my discomfort.

I got exactly what I wanted from him, so I suppose a little embarrassment is the least of what I should expect in the aftermath. I can handle it, or so I tell myself.

"What's up with you tonight, Honey?" Julie asks when she comes over to me with Lauren and Scarlett in tow. Julie was well and truly surprised by the party and has been glowing with excitement ever since her arrival a short time ago. I'm happy to see her that way after months of profound depression following a miscarriage last Christmas.

"Nothing's up with me other than your big three-oh."

"You seem distracted. Is everything all right at the studio?"

"Everything is great, except for the mom-zillas that interfere every step of the way."

"I'm never going to be like that," Julie says.

"I'm beginning to think there's something in the placenta that turns perfectly rational women into lunatics after they procreate."

The girls laugh at that.

"You might be on to something there," Scarlett says. Being my next-door neighbor in town, she hears most of my horror stories soon after they take place.

"Speaking of placenta," Julie says tentatively, taking a look around to make sure no one else can hear her. "I'm pregnant." She says it softly, as if saying it out loud might somehow jinx her.

Knowing how badly she and Matt want to have children, my eyes immediately fill with happy tears. "That's the best news ever." I hug her, and when I pull back from her, I see tears in her eyes, too.

"I've been dying to tell you guys," she says as Lauren and Scarlett hug her, "but Matt and I wanted to wait until we were past the three-month mark before we told anyone this time."

"We won't say anything," I assure her.

"Mum's the word," Lauren says, "or should it be *Mom's the word* in this case?"

She giggles and wipes away a stray tear. "Either way, I appreciate your discretion. We're only telling our immediate families and closest friends. I think Matt is telling Blake now."

I can't *not* look, even though my better judgment is telling me not to make eye contact. Of course I don't listen to my better judgment—remember the *I want you to fuck me* thing from last night? The second I give in to the overwhelming need to look at him, he glances my way, and our gazes connect across the crowded room. And then he starts coming toward me, edging his way through one group after another until he's standing right in front of me.

As if they recognize the man who made them sing last night, my girl parts go crazy, dancing around trying to get his attention.

"You okay?" he asks in a low intimate tone that has the girls singing hallelujah.

"Of course I am. Why do you ask?"

"You seem... I don't know... Rattled or something."

I absolutely hate that he could tell that from across a crowded room.

"Not at all," I say breezily. "Why would I be?"

Rather than answer, he only stares at me. His blue-eyed gaze is so intense, I feel like he's seeing right through me and my fake breeziness.

The stare-fest ends when Matt calls for more ice.

"I'll get it." I head for the freezer in the garage and am piling bags of ice on the garage floor when Blake appears next to me.

Without making eye contact—and thank goodness for that—he

says, "Leave your back door unlocked tonight." He picks up the bags of ice, hoists them to his shoulder and goes back inside while I stand with my mouth hanging open. Only the icy air from the freezer swirling in my face keeps me from overheating.

Did he really just say that? One-and-done Blake Dempsey wants round two? Well, isn't this an unprecedented development...

Blake

I have no idea why I told Honey to leave her door open for me. Okay, that's not entirely true. It's because she seemed rattled, and I'm worried about her. Yeah, you heard me right. I'm actually concerned that something we did last night isn't sitting well with her, and I need to know for sure. Thus my highly unusual request that she leave her door unlocked.

Ugh, what am I doing? I don't get involved. I don't "worry" about my sexual partners after we do the deed. I never make promises I can't keep, and I never, ever, *ever* do entanglements with women.

I have no plans to change my rules with Honey. It's just that underneath her sassy *I want you to fuck me* exterior, she's fragile. And oh my goodness, she'd hate me for thinking that. Honey would never want anyone to think of her as fragile, but I know her well enough to know the cocky attitude she brought into that bar last night is not the real Honey Carmichael. Not even kinda.

No, the real Honey has been trying to overcome her difficult beginnings her entire life by overcompensating with too many men, always searching for that elusive "something" she's never had. I once heard some guys in town speculate that she has a "daddy complex," whatever that is. I promptly shut that down and told them I'd better never hear them talk trash or anything else about her again. I nearly came to blows with one guy who didn't like me telling him what to do. Whatever. No one was going to talk that way about Honey in front of me and get away with it.

The reminder of that incident in the context of what happened last night makes me feel out of sorts and off my game. Of course I'm protective of her. I pinched her on the playground. That's how long I've known her. I'd do the same thing for Lauren or Julie or Scarlett or any of the other girls we grew up with.

A pang in the usually numb center of my chest makes a liar out of me. If I'm being entirely honest, Honey is different from the others. She's always been different, from the time I was pinching her until last night, when I finally got the chance to touch her the way I've wanted to for as long as I can remember... She's been different.

Way back when, and we're talking sixth and seventh grade here, I thought Honey might turn out to be my girlfriend, but that didn't happen. Then Jordan moved to town the summer between eighth and ninth grade, and I never looked at or thought about another girl in the years I was with her. We had plans. Lots and lots of plans. I stopped making plans after I lost her. What was the point? Life will fuck with you no matter what you have planned, so why bother?

At least I'm aware of the fact that I'm a fucked-up mess of a man who appears to function well on the outside. My successful contracting business is proof of my ability to fake it till I make it. I do everything I can for the men who work for me, for my parents, who still live in town, for my siblings, who are all married with kids, for Jordan's parents and for the friends I've managed to hang on to in the twelve years since my heart stopped beating normally.

But on the inside, where I live with myself and my regrets and memories so painful I can't bear to revisit them, I'm a disaster. A no-good, broken-down mess, and I own that. It's why I don't let women get too close to me. It's why I don't get involved. I refuse to risk more than I can afford to lose. I've learned the hard way that it's just not worth the agony when it all goes wrong. And it *always* goes wrong.

How else to explain why smart, beautiful, happy, always upbeat Jordan is lying in a hole in the ground while so many horrible people are allowed to roam this earth? In the beginning, the only way I could cope with the loss was to frequently drink my way to full-on blackout. I quickly learned that I still had to wake up the next day and confront the loss while feeling like total hell. I stopped that before my parents and siblings made good on their threat to hold an intervention and then cart me off to rehab. Now I'm a one-or-two-maybe-three-on-Saturdays beer drinker who rarely overindulges anymore.

No matter what I do, the unrelenting pain never lets me forget. I see Jordan's death as my cross to bear. She died. I lived. The pain is the least of what I owe her.

During the first few unbearable years, everyone in my life urged me to move on. They told me it's what she'd want, and I knew they were right. I've always known that's what she'd want for me, but I've never been able to actually do it. After five years, my friends and family blessedly stopped trying to fix me up with their single friends and colleagues and sisters "who'd be perfect for me."

I'm sure they were all nice girls, but I refuse to inflict myself or my demons on anyone. It simply wouldn't be fair. So there I was, going along with my life, such as it is, when Honey Carmichael came strolling into my favorite bar and made me an offer I couldn't refuse even if I knew at the time that I probably should.

I've had a lot of meaningless, get-my-rocks-off-and-move-on sex since I finally got past that first awful time with someone else. I'm well aware of my reputation around town as a "machine" in the sack, and the women I've been with always comment about the size of my equipment. Whatever.

Without fail, they always come back for more.

I always say no. One and done. That's how I roll. So what in the ever-loving fuck am I doing telling Honey to leave her door unlocked?

Tipping the bottle back, I take a long drink of beer as I watch her across the room, laughing and talking with Julie and Lauren and Scarlett and other women we've known all our lives. Why can't I stop looking at her? Why do I have to notice that her lips are still swollen from last night and there's a hint of razor burn—my razor burn—on her neck from the middle of the night, when my beard started to come back? Why does knowing I left my mark on her in more ways than one give me such a perverse thrill?

Why do I care that she's rattled?

"Having a good time?"

I look up at Matt, my best friend since first grade and the man who single-handedly saved my life in every possible way after Jordan died by not leaving my side for two whole months. "A great time. You done good. Julie seems thrilled."

"It's nice to see her smile again."

I was one of the very few people who knew they were pregnant again after the heartbreaking miscarriage last winter. See what I mean? Life always fucks you up the ass no matter how happy you might be. Their miscarriage is a classic example. What did they do to deserve that devastating blow? Nothing. Absolutely nothing. This sort of thing is why I believe it's easier not to get involved than to risk that kind of pain.

"It sure is," I reply, hiding my inner turmoil from him with the expertise I've perfected over the years.

"Why you staring at Honey?"

Oh shit. "What? I'm not staring at her."

"Um, yeah, you are, and I heard a little rumor that you left the bar with her last night. Any truth to that?"

I can lie to some people—and I'm not ashamed to say I lie shame-lessly when it suits my best interests of staying free and clear of anything that can cause me additional grief—but I've never been able to lie to Matt. "Maybe. She came by. We hung out. Nothing to get wound up about."

"You and Honey Carmichael 'hung out,' and that's nothing to get wound up about?" He snorts with laughter and takes a drink from his beer. "Whatever you say, man."

His comment strikes a note of panic deep inside me, in a place I keep walled off with concrete and barbed wire. "What's that supposed to mean?"

"Nothing. Nothing at all."

Have I mentioned that my best friend often makes me want to throat-punch him? And did I mention that he's one of the two foremen at work who keep my business running smoothly? So punching him isn't an option unless I want to compound my aggrava-tion. "If you've got something to say, just say it. Otherwise, fuck off."

The bastard laughs again, takes another sip of beer and then looks me dead in the eye. "Don't do to her what you usually do, Blake. She means too much to all of us, and you know as well as I do she's not as tough and ballsy as she'd like us to believe. You hurt her, you hurt us."

Fucking hell... "I'm not doing anything with her." Well, if you don't count fucking like rabbits, but that's over now. We did it. It was done. As in past tense. Nothing to worry about.

But there's an ache in my chest that won't go away since I woke up alone this morning after one of the best nights I've had since Jordan died. I took some Tums earlier, hoping that would help, but it didn't make a dent. Maybe I should go to urgent care to see if something is up with my heart. I rub a hand over my chest.

"I mean it, Blake. Don't fuck with her, or you'll answer to me."

Under normal circumstances, I love that our work relationship hasn't gotten in the way of our lifelong friendship. I like that he'll say something like that to me even though I'm technically his boss. But these are not normal circumstances, and tonight, for whatever reason, his words don't roll off me the way they usually do.

"Don't worry about it."

"I will worry about it, and you should, too."

"I hear you, Matt, but there's no need for threats. Honey and I are cool."

At least I hope we are. I'll see to that later when I drop by to check on her. We'll put things back on track, and that will be that. Whoever said sex has to change everything has never met me. I'm a machine. I don't let my emotions into the equation. Ever.

CHAPTER SIX

Honey

I'm a nervous wreck. I have been since that moment in Matt and Julie's garage when Blake told me to leave my door unlocked. What could he possibly want? It couldn't be more sex, because everyone knows he doesn't do more than one night with any woman. Lauren was a rare exception, but that was when he was much younger. In recent years, his one-and-done philosophy has become well known around here.

So that takes me back to the what-could-he-possibly-want question.

I get home around eleven thirty. Blake was still at the party when I left, so I have no idea when to expect him. I go to the back door and stare at the lock for a long moment before I turn the knob to unlock it. The popping sound of the lock disengaging is louder than it has ever been, echoing through my quiet house like a shotgun blast.

Okay, that might be a little dramatic, but everything about this situation feels dramatic to me. Not that I have a lot of experience with drama when it comes to men. They're never much of a mystery to me, and I don't get close enough to any of them to care about what they do.

So why do I care so much about why Blake wants to see me tonight?

Leaving the door unlocked, I walk—or rather limp—into my bedroom and change into a tank top and pajama pants. The bath helped with the aches and pains, but my body is still feeling the aftereffects of my crazy night with Blake. I stop short between my bedroom and the bathroom when the telltale tingling between my legs indicates that, while I might be confused about what he wants, my body knows exactly what *it* wants.

"No way," I say out loud, as if that might toughen my resolve. "No matter what he's got on his mind, there's no way *that's* happening again. I'll never walk again if he touches me tonight."

Today has reminded me all too much of what I felt like after the first time I had sex, with Randy Dade behind his father's barn the summer before my junior year of high school. He went at me like a battering ram, and I was sore for days afterward. I had to tell my Gran that I fell while getting off my horse to explain why I couldn't walk right. I'm not sure if she believed me, but I never had sex with Randy again, much to his dismay.

I didn't have sex again for two years after that traumatizing incident, and the next time wasn't so bad. Neither was the time after that. But it was never anything special until I did it with Blake. And of course, the one time it was something other than just okay, it had to be with the one guy who will never want anything more.

"You knew the score going into that bar last night, Honey Carmichael," I say to myself in the mirror. "Don't bullshit a bullshitter, and don't blow up one night into something more than it was. *Just. Sex.*"

This is exactly what Lauren warned me against—going all soft in the middle over a man who'd never want softness from me or any other woman. It would do me good to remember that. I'll see what he wants tonight and send him on his way, hoping I don't see him again for a while, until I have time to tuck our encounter into a box in my mind and put it in the past where it belongs. I can do that. I *have* to do that.

A few minutes later, the latch on the back door clicks when it opens, and my heart nearly bursts from the adrenaline and excitement and... *Oh for goodness sake, Honey, stop it. Stop it right now.* I gather myself by taking a couple of deep breaths, and then I leave the bathroom, cut through my bedroom and enter what Gran always referred to as the "parlor," the room she kept pristine for guests. Blake is standing in the middle of it with his hands on his hips and a scowl on his face.

His gaze goes directly to my breasts, which fill out my tank top rather well. The shirt might've been a mistake in hindsight, but while he checks me out, his scowl morphs into something... hungrier. That's the only word I can think of to describe what I see in the heated look he gives me.

"You wanted to see me?" I ask, sounding far too breathless for my liking.

"Yeah, I did."

I'm about to ask him why when his hands fall from his hips and he comes to me. It takes everything I have not to back away from him, to remember this is Blake, my lifelong friend and one-time lover. I have nothing to fear from him. But as he comes closer and the hunger turns ravenous, I realize I have every reason in the world to fear him and the power I've given him to hurt me. "W-what did you need?"

His hands land on my hips, and he jerks me toward him. "This."

I crash into his chest and squeak with surprise. I look up to ask him what the hell he's doing, but I never get the chance because his lips come down on mine in a kiss that takes me right back to last night and the sublime pleasure I found in his arms.

Later, I'll have the time to process this and to wonder how I went from resolved to his tongue in my mouth in four seconds flat, but right now I've got all I can do to handle my body's reaction to his touch. Fireworks. That's the best word I can use to describe how it feels when he touches me. Tiny explosions that erupt under my skin, making my nipples tighten and my clit ache with desire.

His arms wrap around me, making me his prisoner, not that I mind.

No one has ever kissed me the way Blake does, and I was a fool to think one night would be enough for either of us. I want to climb on him, wrap my legs around his waist and grind myself against the hard cock that presses into my belly.

He does that mind-reading thing again when he cups my ass and lifts me without missing a beat in the kiss. I wrap myself around him and tip my head to the right to improve the angle. His groan tells me he approves. Many minutes later, he breaks the kiss and turns his attention to my neck.

"I promised myself I wouldn't touch you tonight." He bites the tendon at the base of my neck, and I almost come from the jolt of electricity that travels directly to my clit. "I'm no good for you, Honey. You deserve so much better."

"You're good for me right now." I fist a handful of his hair and drag him into another kiss. I can't control the need to grind my sex on his cock, and he can't seem to control the need to grind right back. If not for his jeans and my pajamas, we'd be having actual sex rather than the simulated kind.

"One more time," he says in that raspy, sexy voice that will fuel my fantasies for the rest of my life after this momentous weekend. "Tell me you understand."

"One more time."

"And that's all. Do we agree?"

"Yes, Blake. We agree."

I realize we're moving when we cross the threshold into my bedroom and he comes down on top of me on my bed, all while continuing to thrust his tongue into my mouth with increasing desperation.

I'm right there with him, every bit as desperate for him as he is for me.

He breaks the kiss only long enough to pull my pajama pants off and shed his T-shirt and jeans. Dear God, he's commando under there, and his big cock is so hard, the tip is purple.

My mouth waters, and I sit up to reach for him. "Let me," I say when he would've moved out of my reach. I wrap my hand around the base of his cock and begin to stroke him as I take him into my mouth, sucking the broad head and lashing it with my tongue.

The sound he makes is nothing short of feral, and it sets me on fire for him. I force myself to focus on the task at hand, which is bringing him as much pleasure as he's brought me. With that in mind, I take him as deeply into my mouth as I can, sucking and licking and stroking him until he butts up against my throat. I work through the impulse to gag, and he slips into my throat.

"Fuck, Honey," he growls as he pumps his hips. "Don't stop. Don't ever stop."

My eyes water and tears fall down my cheeks as I concentrate on breathing through my nose while my fingers travel down to stroke his balls, which are almost as hard as his cock.

He gasps. "Let me go, darlin'. Now."

Wondering if I did something wrong, I withdraw from him slowly, running my tongue up the length of his shaft before letting him pop free of my mouth. "Did I not do it right?"

"If you did it any more right, I would've passed out." His hands curve under my knees, and he tugs me to the edge of the mattress, aligning his cock against my pussy and giving a shove that makes me scream—and not in a good way. "Ah fuck, you're sore." He pulls back and drops to his knees by the bed, leaning in to lick my sensitive, pulsating flesh.

I nearly weep from the sweet way he makes love to me with gentle strokes of his tongue over my clit and then down to my tender opening. I know I shouldn't be shocked when he goes even lower, licking me in places no one had ever touched me before last night. I come in slow, easy waves, one orgasm folding into the next, my entire body caught up in the pleasure.

The minute it finally ends, he starts all over again, keeping up the slow, gentle theme with his tongue but raising his hands to my breasts to pinch my nipples just hard enough that I feel the reaction everywhere.

"Blake... I want..."

"What, darlin'? What do you want?"

"You inside me."

"You're too sore."

"Go slow. I want it so bad." I feel empty and needy and desperate for a man for the first time in my life. And not just any man. *This* man.

Standing upright, he stares down at me, and I can only imagine how I must look with my hair wild around my head, my legs splayed open, my nipples standing on end and a desperate need pulsing through me. Apparently, he likes what he sees, because his face lifts into the half smile that makes my heart ache for the happy, carefree boy he was before life taught him the cruelest of lessons.

I hold out my arms to him, and he comes down on top of me, aligning his cock to my opening and giving a gentle thrust. Thanks to his efforts, I'm so wet that he slides in easier than before. It burns more than hurts as my flesh stretches to accommodate him.

"Ah, God, Honey, you're so tight."

"In the past, that hasn't been a good thing."

He raises his head to look down at me. "Why not?"

"I couldn't always, you know, get it in." I'm on fire with mortification, but in for a penny... "And I've never been with anyone as big as you are."

"They didn't take the time to make sure you were ready."

"They also didn't turn me on the way you do."

"Is that so?"

I bite my lip and nod as he continues to enter me in short little thrusts, retreating each time.

"Ready for more?"

"I-I think so."

"Nice and easy, darlin'. Nice and easy."

True to his word, it takes a long time for him to enter me fully, and when he finally does, we're both sweating and breathing hard and on the verge of release.

"Wait," he whispers, his lips brushing up against my ear and restarting the wildfire inside me. "Slow it down."

"If we go any slower, it'll be morning before we finish."

"Is that a bad thing?"

I moan and squirm and tighten my internal muscles—everything I can think of to get things—especially him—moving. But he's in no rush, and I swear his cock is getting bigger with every second he spends inside me.

"You feel like heaven, Honey." His lips skim over mine in a fleeting caress. "Feels so good. Tell me it's good for you, too."

"It is. I love it." I grasp his tight ass and sink my fingernails into his flesh, begging him for sweet relief as I push my hips against him.

"Ah, baby, you drive a hard bargain."

I gasp with laughter. "I think the *hard* bargain is all you."

"Nah, darlin', it's all you." He begins to move—finally—stroking in and out of me slowly and gently, being careful not to hurt me. I'll still feel this tomorrow because of his sheer size. He's way more than I'm used to. "Fold your hands behind my neck."

Uncertain of why he wants me to do that, I slide my hands around him and clasp them together.

"Hold on tight." With his hands under me, he picks me up and brings me down on him, his cock wedging even deeper inside me—so deep that I gasp from the sensations that spiral from the place we're joined to everywhere else. He moves me slowly up and down, our flesh slick and our breathing rough. "So good, Honeydew melon. So fucking good."

"Yes," I laugh at his latest name for me and cry out the single word, my head falling back as he takes me on a slow ride to heaven. Nothing has ever felt so good. I'm wise enough to know that nothing will ever again feel quite this good. What a profoundly depressing thought. But I told him I understood, and I do. I know what he's capable of—and what he isn't. This will have to be enough.

If we only have this second bonus night, never to be repeated, I intend to enjoy every minute of it.

Blake

It's good with her. I feel it, and I know she does, too. There's something to be said for doing this with someone I've known forever and feel safe with. I can let go with her and be myself. I don't have to hide the agony I carry with me every second of every day. She knows. She was there. I don't have to explain anything to her, and that's a huge relief.

My brain, which runs on full speed every minute that I'm awake, gives me a break when I'm with her. I have something else to think about besides regrets and remorse and relentless grief. Staying so busy I don't have time to breathe is a coping mechanism that's worked well for me over the years.

But fucking Honey works better.

She looks up at me with those bottomless eyes, and I lose myself in her.

The guys I work with say I'm a machine because of how much I get done in an average day. I don't ask them to do anything I'm not willing to do, too. I push myself harder than anyone, and the result is a very successful business that gets bigger every year. For all I care about success.

The women I spend time with call me a machine in bed because of my stamina and because I'm "emotionally remote," as one of them said. If that makes me a machine, I can live with that more easily than I could live with an emotional involvement.

Staying removed has worked for me, and even with Honey Carmichael's silky-soft skin wrapped around me, I'm not about to change my mind about that. But I do love the way she looks at me when I'm inside her—part awe, part confusion, part affection.

I cling to the affection. I hadn't realized how badly I needed it until Honey showed me what I've been missing by powering through life, one meaningless encounter at a time. The affection is what brought me to her tonight for one more dose of her special brand of sweetness.

She's so tight and wet and hot that I'm on the verge of release way too soon, so I withdraw from her, enjoying her little squeak of protest. I bend my head to take her left nipple into my mouth while pinching the right one between my fingers. Kissing my way down the front of her, I lift her legs to my shoulders and open her to my tongue.

"Sweetest honey I've ever tasted."

Her thighs tighten around my head, and I lose myself in her. The only thing I care about is making her come harder than she ever has before. I want to leave my mark on her. I want her to remember this after it's over. Why I want that is something I can think about later, when I'm back to being alone again. Right now, I have far better things to concern myself with than returning to my empty, hyper-regimented life.

I draw her clit into my mouth and suck hard, running my tongue back and forth over the tight little nub while pushing my fingers into her at the same time. The combination has the desired effect, and she erupts with a cry of pleasure that travels right to my hard cock. He wants in on this right fucking now.

She's still coming when I push into her, triggering a second orgasm on top of the first one. Her fingers dig into my ass when she pulls me deeper into her. As I pound into her, she raises her hips to meet my every stroke. We move together like longtime lovers, a thought that causes me to lose my rhythm for a second.

Of course she notices. "Are you okay?"

"Yeah, darlin', I'm good. You?"

"Mmm. Yes, I'm good."

I smile down at her. "Sweetest Bit-O-Honey I ever had."

She returns my smile and buries her fingers in my hair, drawing me into a kiss that's so sweet and tender, I begin to ache on the inside for what can never be. If only I were different. If only I were capable... But I'm not, and wishing for things that can never be is a surefire path to madness.

I know myself, and I have no doubt I'm better off maintaining the status quo than deviating from the course that has kept me sane all these years. But I'll confess that I'm tempted to want more for the first time since Jordan died—and that scares the living hell out of me.

"Fuck, Honey..." I start to withdraw from her. "I forgot a condom."

She stops me. "I'm on birth control, and I'm clean."

"I am, too. I haven't been with anyone in a long time." I pick up the pace, driving myself relentlessly and taking her with me. "God, this feels so good."

She comes again, and the tight clamp of her pussy on my cock finishes me off. I come hard and land on her afterward when my arms won't hold me up any longer. I worry that I'm crushing her, but she doesn't seem to mind. Her fingers comb through my hair in a sweet, calming caress that has me relaxing into her embrace.

My eyes are heavy from the night without sleep. I should get up and go home. Spending the night isn't part of my program, but I decide a few more minutes won't hurt anything.

CHAPTER SEVEN

Blake

The next thing I know, it's morning. Sunshine is streaming through the blinds in Honey's bedroom, and the smell of coffee and bacon makes my stomach growl. *Fuck*. I spent the night. I check my watch and see that it's after ten o'clock. I can't recall the last time I slept that late.

Wait... Yes, I can. A poignant memory resurfaces so suddenly it takes my breath away. My mom waking me up at noon to tell me that Jordan was trying to call me to come get her to swim in our pool. Her car was in the shop, and I'd been driving her around all week. Groaning at being awakened, I dragged myself out of bed to go get her and brought her to my house to swim.

All these years later, I can still remember the white bikini she wore and how it offset her dark tan. Jordan's mother was Mexican and had passed down her dark hair and skin to her gorgeous daughter.

My mom made us lunch and then left for a hair appointment. The second her car pulled out of the driveway, we ran for my room, where we spent the next two hours making love before I took her home to babysit her younger brothers. We were hit by an eighteen-wheeler four blocks from my house and six blocks from hers. I never saw it coming.

The memory sears me, making me ache all over and reminding me why I don't do sleepovers, why I don't get involved, why I don't do commitment or anything other than power through each day to lose myself to the blessed oblivion that only sleep usually provides, until the nightmares intrude to plunge me back into the darkness.

Running from the past and the pain and the grief is exhausting, but I've yet to figure out a better coping mechanism. Staring up at Honey's ceiling, I run my fingers through my hair, wishing there was a way to scrub certain memories from my brain. It's ironic that I have no memory of the accident or the immediate aftermath, but I vividly remember every minute I spent with Jordan. I remember the sweet joy of first love and the horrific, excruciating agony of being told she was gone.

I shudder at the memory of my parents standing by my hospital bed, both of them in tears as they broke the news to me.

And why the fuck am I thinking about this shit now? Angry with myself, I get up and help myself to Honey's shower. I get dressed with the intention of leaving as fast as I can without being rude.

In the kitchen, Honey is wearing a T-shirt that just covers her bare ass. Her hair is up in a bun, and she's singing a country song I don't recognize in the pure sweet voice that takes me back to her years as a singer in a local band. Standing watch over a pan on the stove, she's so damned cute and sexy at the same time. A strange feeling twists inside me, filling me with yearning. For what, I couldn't say, but whatever it is involves her.

"Hungry?" she asks when she spies me watching her.

"I could eat." Wait, where did that come from? I was going to leave. "It smells good."

She gestures to the barstools at the counter. "Have a seat."

I'll leave after breakfast. She went to all this trouble. It'd be lame of me not to eat the food she cooked, and I am hungry. The eggs are light and fluffy, the bacon perfectly cooked and the toast already buttered for me. She slides a mug of coffee fixed just the way I like it—cream and two sugars—across the counter before she joins me on the next stool.

She's given me twice as much as she served herself. The metaphor isn't lost on me. She came to me the other night wanting to be with a man who knew how to please a woman. But could she possibly know what her sweet affection has done for me?

Suddenly, I don't want this to be over, but how do I tell her that? I want more—of her, of the affection, of the amazing sex and the tenderness. Panic wells in my chest, and I'm breathless with longing. Blood pumps furiously through my reawakened heart like it's a deadened limb coming back to life. I *feel* something for Honey, something I haven't felt for anyone since Jordan died.

But how do I change the rules that I set? I puzzle over this quandary while I enjoy a second cup of coffee. "I have to drive out to a job site this afternoon." The words pour forth before I take the time to consider the potential consequences. "You feel like taking a ride?"

She looks over at me, clearly surprised by my offer. "Sure." To her credit, she doesn't remind me that I told her, just last night, that whatever this is between us would be over today.

I'm enormously relieved by her one-word answer—and to know there will be more time with her. How much? I can't say, but right now, I'll settle for more.

Honey

He was quiet at breakfast, so his invitation takes me by surprise. I assumed he was trying to figure out a way to bow out gracefully. Instead, he was apparently thinking about asking me to go somewhere with him.

Interesting. It takes some effort on my part not to show him he's shocked me. I sense I need to tread lightly with him or scare him off. After spending the last two nights with him, I don't want to scare him off. That's the opposite of what I want, but I know how he rolls, so I'm trying not to overthink his simple invitation, even though I know there's nothing "simple" about it.

"Let me just grab a quick shower," I say after I finish loading the dishwasher.

Blake comes up behind me, wraps his arms around me and kisses the curve of my neck. That's all it takes to make me wish he'd invited me back to bed rather than to his job site. "Thank you for breakfast. It was really good."

"Oh. You're welcome."

His hands move from my hips under my T-shirt to my ribs and up to cup my breasts.

My nipples immediately tighten, and the ache begins anew in my pussy. I should be too sore after what we did last night to want more, but that doesn't stop me from pushing my ass back against his hard cock.

He gasps and pinches my nipples.

"Are you in a huge rush to get to your job site?"

"I've got all day, darlin'."

"Could we, I mean, if you want to, that is—" I let out an inelegant squeak when he lifts me right off my feet and walks us into my bedroom, putting me face down on my bed. "Blake—"

"Like this," he says gruffly as he unzips his fly. He tests my readiness by running the tip of his cock through the dampness between my legs. "God, you're always so wet for me, Honeydew."

I raise my hips, hoping to encourage him to get on with it. He doesn't need much encouragement.

"How do you want it? Hard and fast or slow and sweet?"

No man has ever asked me that before, and I'm struck by the realization that I'm slowly becoming addicted to the way *this* man makes love or fucks or whatever it is we're doing here.

"Honey?"

"Hard and fast."

"Are you sore?"

"A little."

"Then let's start out slow and easy."

True to his word, he enters me from behind in slow but steady thrusts, giving my body time to stretch to accommodate him. He's so big and so hard that the burn is inevitable, but it quickly gives way to pleasure. Grasping my hips, he pumps into me as my nipples rub against the quilt on my bed. I fist a handful of the quilt because I need to hold on to something when he picks up the pace.

I cry out in surprise when an orgasm hits me while he's deep inside me.

"Ah fuck," he groans, surging into me as he comes. "You make me lose all control when that tight pussy clamps down on me."

"You make me lose control with that huge cock of yours."

He grunts out a laugh. "Glad you like it."

"I'm quickly becoming addicted to it." I no sooner say that than I wish I could take it back. He doesn't want me addicted to any part of him.

"I can live with that," he whispers, biting down on my earlobe before withdrawing from me. He gives me a playful swat on the butt. "You got me all dirty again, so let's hit the shower and head out before I forget I've got stuff to do and drag you back to bed."

Am I allowed to say that I wouldn't object to being dragged back to bed by him? Maybe I'll save that for another time, if there is one.

He joins me in the shower and seems to take great pleasure in thoroughly washing every inch of me with lemongrass soap.

"I love the smell of that soap," he says.

"I get it from Marfa Brands in town."

"Good stuff."

"I'll get you some."

I'm once again fully aroused as if I didn't just have a huge orgasm ten minutes ago. How does he do that? I hook my arms around his neck and draw him into a kiss that quickly escalates. I'm never insatiable like this with men. Usually, I'm a one-and-done kind of gal, but Blake is showing me a side to myself I didn't know existed. And when he lifts me off my feet and once again impales me on that huge cock, I realize he's ruining me for all other men one crazy fuck at a time.

And this is absolutely crazy! We just did it, and now we're doing it again. I'm powerless to resist him as he controls my slow slide down his rigid shaft.

"Blake." I'm breathless with desire and full to the brim with his hard, throbbing flesh.

A shudder travels through his entire body. "Hold on tight. This is gonna be really, really fast."

He's completely unhinged as he presses me against the tile wall in the shower and goes at me like he hasn't gotten laid in a year. All I can do is hold on tight and enjoy the ride. His fingers dig into my ass cheeks, which he holds open to better the angle.

"Honey... God, Honey... So good." His face tightens from the strain, and when his thumb finds my clit, I explode.

He comes with a roar that drowns out the sound of the shower. And then he's kissing me again, like a madman or maybe like a man who is finally feeling something other than grief for the first time in years.

"Holy hell," he mutters. "I've never had sex without condoms with anyone else."

"You like it?"

"If I liked it any more, I'd be dead."

I might be giving myself too much credit, but he seems different after the time we've spent together, lighter maybe, and I begin to hope—

No. Just no. Remember what Lauren told you. You're not going to find your home with him. That may still be true, but whatever this is with him, it feels pretty damned good for right now.

———

IT'S AFTER NOON BY THE TIME WE FINALLY WEAR OURSELVES OUT and remember that we were going to drive out to one of his job sites. My brain is completely scrambled from orgasms. I wanted to know what the big deal was, and now I know. I get why sex makes people do crazy things like while away an entire Sunday morning in bed, in the shower and back in bed.

My body is still humming from the workout as I sit in the passenger seat of Blake's truck, singing along to "Free Bird" on the classic-rock station he has on the radio.

"God, this song," I say. "Takes me right back to high school and the band."

"You guys were good."

"Those were some fun times."

"You ever talk about getting back together?"

"Once in a while there'll be a group text, usually around the holidays when everyone is home, but we never seem to make it happen."

"I thought you'd do something with your singing."

"So did I."

"Why didn't you?"

It's hard for me to talk about that time in my life, when I traded my dream for the woman who gave me everything. "You may not remember, but I was a voice major at Juilliard in New York when Gran got sick." I shrug, as if the memories of that time aren't still as painful now as they were then. "I left school to come home to care for her, and I never went back."

"How come?"

I choose my words carefully. "Losing her was a very tough thing for me. It messed me up for a long time."

"She was all you had."

"Yeah." She's been gone ten long years, and I've yet to feel as at home with anyone as I did with her. Thank God for Lauren, Julie and Scarlett and the rest of my friends who do their best to fill the void, but nothing and no one can ever replace the person who loved me best of all.

We drive past El Cosmico, a Marfa institution. The vast eclectic campground offers guests everything from "luxurious" Airstream campers to Sioux-style teepees to Mongolian yurts.

"The campground is busy this weekend," Blake comments.

"There's a festival at the Chinati," I say, referring to one of the two foundations in town started to maintain the legacy of the late Marfa artist Donald Judd. He brought the arts culture to the town in the 1970s with his installations and non-museums where art was permanently displayed rather than cycled in and out.

Judd's patronage of the arts in our town is a big reason my Desert Babies business has done so well. People come from all over to our isolated little town in West Texas to experience the art culture. In addition to my booming Desert Babies business, I sell a lot of desert landscapes, and my photographs of the Marfa Mystery Lights are some of my bestsellers.

"How'd you go from majoring in vocal performance to running a photography studio?" Blake asks.

"That evolved from what had been a hobby in school. When Gran was sick, I'd take advantage of every chance I got to get out when her friends would come stay with her. I'd drive out to the desert and take pictures for hours. It was the only way I could relax. By the time she died, I had a lot of work ready to go. I used some of the money she left me to lease the studio, and then almost ten years went by without me realizing it."

"Life happens."

"Something like that."

"I did sort of the same thing when I finally made it to college."

He didn't have to tell me about the football scholarship to Texas A&M he ended up turning down because of the injuries he suffered in the accident that killed Jordan. The whole town knew about that.

"The minute they sprang me from the rehab hospital, I did a semester at UT in Austin, found out college wasn't for me and went to work for my uncle. I bought him out when he was ready to retire. Like you said, ten years went by, and here I am."

"Are you where you want to be?"

"I guess. I can't imagine doing any other kind of work or being stuck in an office all day." He shudders. "That would kill me. Garrett already wants to kill me half the time because I suck at keeping track of receipts and expenses and other crap that gets his panties in a wad."

"Lauren wants to date him." The words are out of my mouth before I take even one second to contemplate the magnitude of what I'm doing.

Blake glances over at me. "Is that so?"

I'm struck by how gorgeous he is, with a sprinkling of golden whiskers on his jaw, lips swollen from kissing me and eyes as blue as the endless Texas sky. "I shouldn't have said anything. Speaking of someone wanting to kill me."

"Might be info he'd like to have."

"As long as my name isn't attached to that info."

"Your secret is safe with me, darlin'."

I shouldn't want to swoon at him calling me that. Texas men call all the females in their lives darlin'. But coming from him to me... Well, it's a good thing I'm sitting down. "Where're we going anyway?" We're on 67 South, heading toward Presidio.

"Just a little further." That's all he says, so I settle in to watch the world go by in our remote corner of the state. We're hours from El Paso to the northwest, Austin to the east and San Antonio to the southeast. There're not a lot of places we can go in this direction without ending up at the Mexican border.

Most of the time, I love the isolation of Marfa. I love my small town with the artsy flair and the tourists who come for music festivals and art events that happen throughout the year. There's always something going on in town, which keeps it from getting boring.

The song "Sex Machine" by James Brown comes on the radio, and I lose it laughing.

"What's so funny?" Blake asks, a smile tugging at the corners of his mouth.

"This song." I fan my face and dab at the laughter tears in my eyes.

"What about it?"

"I can't tell you."

"Don't worry. I already know that's what they say about me."

I'm horrified. "*How* do you know that?"

He shrugs. "I've always known. It's no big deal. Hell, it's true."

I'm oddly, strangely hurt for him. "It's not true," I say quietly.

"Why do you say that?"

"There's so much more to you than *that*."

"Not that much more. Not anymore."

Not since he lost Jordan. That's the part he leaves unspoken. Nothing has been the same since he lost her, but he isn't the unfeeling robot he's made himself out to be. I saw cracks in his armor during the two nights I spent with him. I saw it in his expression when he appeared at my door last night, not seeming to understand why he was there or what he wanted from me.

I witnessed his need to connect to another human being. I understand that need better than most ever could. For reasons I can't explain even to myself, I reach across the bench seat for his hand. After a moment's hesitation, he curls his fingers around mine, and we ride that way for another five miles before he takes a right-hand turn onto a dirt road that ends at a construction site. Or rather, a renovation site. Something about the place is familiar to me.

"Where are we?"

"Jordan's grandparents' farm."

"Oh, I remember! There's a swimming hole on the property."

"Yes."

"What're you doing out here?"

"I bought it about a year ago, and I work on it whenever I can."

For some reason, this strikes me as unreasonably sad. I clear the emotion from my throat. "What do you plan to do with it when it's finished?"

"Haven't decided yet. Come take a look."

We get out of the truck, and he waits for me at the front, extending a hand to help me over a log. He doesn't let go once I've safely landed on the other side.

I try not to make too much of this, but I secretly thrill in the excitement of being here with him, of holding his hand, of the connection I found with him in bed, in the shower and sitting next to him at breakfast. Life is a little less lonely with him around, not that I think he's here to stay or anything.

The two-story house used to be gray, but the paint is faded and chipping. We take sagging stairs onto a rickety porch, where he releases my hand to unlock the front door and gestures for me to go in ahead of him. "Careful," he says.

I see why when I get my first look at the inside, which has been completely gutted.

"Let me give you a tour," he says with that small grin. I'm starting to realize that's as much of a smile as he has anymore. Pointing, he says, "Living room/dining room/kitchen all one big open space with a laundry room and half bath off the kitchen. Let's go upstairs." He takes my hand again and leads the way up the stairs.

"Master suite to the right, hall bathroom and two bedrooms at the other end."

We go into the area he's designated as the master suite. It's a mess, but I can see the potential. "This is a great space."

"I think so, too. And the wood floors are original to the house. All the wood will be amazing when it's refinished."

"Why don't you send one of your teams in here to get it done faster?"

"I want to do this one myself, and I'm not in any rush."

"Do Jordan's parents know you bought it?"

"Yeah, I asked them if they minded before I did it. They were thrilled. They said it'd be nice to keep it in the family." He rubs his hand over the exposed wood walls, and I realize this is a labor of love to him.

"That's nice of them."

"They've always been nicer to me than I deserved."

"They don't blame you, Blake. No one does." *Only you*, I want to say, but don't.

He keeps his gaze averted, but I see the tightness in his jaw and face.

"If you ever need help with painting or sanding or anything simple like that... Let me know."

The tension lifts when he looks at me. "I just might do that. Maybe you could take some before-and-after pictures for me."

I smile up at him. "I'd love to."

He looks down at me, his eyes dropping to my lips as he raises a hand to caress my cheek.

I feel that soft touch in every cell of my body.

"You're so very, very pretty, Honeysuckle."

I'm inordinately moved by the compliment, and I absolutely love his endless nicknames for me. "Thank you."

He tilts my chin up and brings his lips down on mine.

I wrap my arms around him and lose myself in the sweet, tender kiss.

Blake backs me up to the exposed wall and presses his lower body against mine as he tilts his head to better the angle of the kiss.

What are we doing? I want to stop everything to ask that question. Why can't we seem to sate this craving for each other? Where has it come from all of a sudden, or was it always there, simmering below the surface every time we were together over the last few years? Is that the reason I was so easily convinced by Lauren to step way out of character and proposition him in a bar? Have I wanted him all along?

I don't have any of the answers to these questions. I just know that I like the way it feels to be held and kissed by him. I like being pinned below him in bed and impaled by his giant cock as he stares down at me with heated blue eyes. I like everything about him, if I'm being truthful, even the darkness that lives within him.

He withdraws from the kiss slowly, stroking his tongue over my bottom lip. His hands are cupping my face, and when I open my eyes, I catch him watching me with heat and hunger in his gaze. "Want to check out the swimming hole?"

"Sure." I'm up for anything that extends our time together. Even as I tell myself not to get attached, that's turning out to be harder than I thought it would be. With every kiss, every touch, every confidence shared, he's working his way under my skin.

CHAPTER EIGHT

Blake

I have no idea what I was thinking, bringing Honey out here. This is a place I shared with Jordan. Honey doesn't belong here. Except, I like having her here. I like showing her the work I've done so far and telling her the plans I have for the rest of the renovations. I like the questions she asks and the interest she shows. I like the way she reached for my hand in the truck when she seemed to know I needed the comfort, and I like how soft her lips are under mine.

She follows me downstairs and through the war zone that will one day be a showplace. I'll see to that, and I'll do it myself. If it takes a year or five years, I'll bring it back to its former glory. Jordan was close to her paternal grandparents, and we spent a lot of time out here visiting them, swimming and looking at the stars on dark Texas nights.

In a weird way, I feel like I'm doing something for her by bringing her grandparents' run-down farmhouse back to life. They're long gone now, both of them dying within a year after they lost her. Though no one has ever said so, I think they died of broken hearts. I can certainly understand how that might be possible.

I shake off those thoughts now and try to focus on the present rather than the past that never leaves me alone for long. "If you want to wait here, I'll grab a blanket out of the truck."

"Sounds good." Honey wraps her hand around one of the new wood beams I installed on the porch to hold up the roof that had been in danger of collapsing when I bought the place. Shoring that up had been the first thing I did after the closing.

I jog the short distance to my truck and grab the blanket I keep alongside my tools in the workbox in the truck bed. Returning to the porch, I hold out a hand to Honey, inviting her to join me. Her gaze locks on mine as she comes down the stairs and takes my outstretched hand.

Why does it feel so damned right to be here with her? To hold her hand? To watch the way her taut, lithe body moves in the lightweight sundress that shows off her exceptional curves? Why does it feel so good to kiss her and hold her and draw strength from her? She's so gutsy and brave, making her way almost completely on her own since she lost her Gran, and I admire her greatly for that.

I don't know what I would've done without my parents and family to prop me up when the load got too heavy for me to carry alone. I never would've survived without them.

Honey hasn't had that support and has thrived anyway. She's never played the "poor me" card or lamented her lack of family. Rather, she's played the hand she was dealt and played it well. I admire her for that, too.

We walk together in easy silence. She doesn't feel the need to fill every second with mindless chatter the way some women do. I add that to the growing list of things I like about her. The swimming hole is about half a mile from the house. I know this because Jordan once convinced me that half a mile is far enough away to make love at the swimming hole. The entire time, I'd been sure her grandfather was going to appear at any moment with a shotgun.

He hadn't, but the fear of that shotgun led to a less than satisfying encounter. The memory makes me smile, which is a welcome relief from the agony I usually feel when I think of her.

"What're you smiling about over there?"

I consider making something up, but then I decide to go with the truth. "I'm thinking about the time Jordan and I came out to the swimming hole right around dusk, after dinner with her grandparents, and she talked me into more than a swim out here. The whole time I was waiting for her grandfather to show up with the shotgun he kept over the door. The fear gave me performance anxiety."

Honey laughs along with me, and by sharing it with her, the memory takes on the sweet feeling of nostalgia rather than the grinding, endless pain of grief. The nostalgia is a welcome relief.

We're sweating from the relentless heat of the midday sun, and the freshwater spring looks incredibly inviting as we approach it. I haven't been out here in years, not since the last time I was here with Jordan. Even when I was thinking about purchasing the twelve-acre spread, I didn't come out here. It was just too painful and raw.

But now, with Honey here with me, it feels new again, like we're creating something from the ashes of what used to be.

Her big brown eyes light up with pleasure at the sight of the water. "I'd forgotten how pretty it is out here."

Fields of wildflowers give the arid landscape a splash of much-needed color.

"It really is." I spread the blanket on the ground next to the water, realizing we aren't going to last long out here in this heat. "I didn't think to grab sunscreen."

"That's okay. I put it on after my shower."

"You did?"

"Yep. That's Gran's training. She was always preaching about protecting my skin from the West Texas sun, as if the sun is more potent here than anywhere else."

"Your skin is lovely." I drag a finger down her arm. "Smooth and soft and the color of honey." I watch her nipples peak under the bodice of her dress, and just that quickly, I'm hard for her again.

"Gran wouldn't be happy about the tan, but I can't seem to

completely avoid the sun, and I wouldn't want to anyway. A girl's gotta live while she takes care of her skin."

"True," I say with a grunt of laughter. "It's kinda hot out here."

"You say that like you didn't know it'd be ninety-something today like it is every day this time of year."

I glance over at her, and her saucy smile does something to me. It penetrates the wall I've put up around myself to keep out anything and everything that could hurt me. Desperate to recover my equilibrium, I tear my gaze off her and look at the water. "Want to swim?"

"I didn't bring a suit."

"Neither did I."

"Oh."

"There's no one around for miles and miles."

"How do you know that?"

"I know how far my property extends and what's on either side of it, which is not much."

She rolls her bottom lip between her teeth, and I can see that she's considering it.

I stand and pull the T-shirt over my head and then extend my hand to help her up. "Double dog dare ya." I haven't said those words or anything even remotely playful to anyone in longer than I can remember. They feel good rolling off my lips. I unbutton my jeans and push them down, kicking them aside.

Honey takes a long, hungry look down my naked body, stopping at my cock, which is so hard it stretches up to my belly button. She licks her lips and shocks the living shit out of me when she drops to her knees to take me into her mouth. Is this the same girl who was just worried about getting caught skinny-dipping?

Fucking hell, that feels good. I let my head fall back as I bury my fingers in her soft, silky hair.

"You have the most beautiful cock in the whole world," she says in a husky, sexy voice that travels straight to my balls in a bolt of electricity that has me on the verge of coming. "So hard and big and long." She strokes me with her hand and tongue, taking me to the edge of insanity before she sucks me in again and nearly finishes me off. I tremble violently, like a boy getting his first blowjob, but she makes everything feel like the first time again.

Lashing me with her tongue, she picks up the pace of her hand on the widest part of my cock.

"Honey... Stop." I pull myself free of her mouth and drop to my knees to kiss her. We fall to the blanket in a tangle of arms and legs. I reach beneath her skirt to find her simple cotton panties soaked through. I groan from the realization that pleasuring me turned her on. Pushing her panties aside, I push two fingers into her wetness as our kiss goes from sweet to fierce in an instant.

This is utter insanity! We've already done it three times today. That would usually take care of me for a week, but it took only an hour for me to want her again. Withdrawing my fingers, I pull her panties down her legs, toss them aside and push into her slowly, carefully, keeping in mind that she has to be sore after our marathon weekend.

Her back bows and her legs fall open in a helpless surrender that goes straight to my heart. Dear God, what is she *doing* to me? Her tight pussy clamps down on the head of my cock, making me see stars. I pull on the top of her dress until her breasts spring free and feast my mouth on her nipples.

This is hot, sweaty, no-holds-barred passion. There's no other word for it as I fight my way past the resistance of her internal muscles to enter her fully. She lets out a keening cry as the widest part of me stretches her to the absolute limit.

"I love your hot, tight pussy," I whisper in her ear.

She whimpers, and her muscles grip me like a glove.

"I love to fuck you, Honey Nut Cheerio."

A gasp of laughter escapes from her clenched jaw.

"Do you love to fuck me, too?"

"*Yes*," she cries. "Yes, I love it."

A low growl comes from somewhere deep inside me as I pick up the pace, hammering into her now, mindless of soreness or the hard ground beneath her or the hot sun on my bare ass or anything other than the exquisite pleasure that overtakes me every time I'm inside her, especially bareback.

I reach under her to grasp her soft ass cheeks and pull them apart to go deeper into her. I press my middle fingers against her anus and let the wetness from her pussy ease the way as I push my fingers into her.

She ignites, screaming as the orgasm hits her hard and fast.

I have to bite my lip to keep from joining her, but I'm not finished with her yet. Not by a long shot. I ride the waves of her orgasm until it finally dies down. Then I withdraw from her so suddenly, she lets out a squeak of surprise. Moving quickly, I turn her over and drag her up to her knees before driving into her again from behind. Now her sweet little ass is right in front of me, and I can watch as I push two fingers into her back door.

Everything inside her goes tight when I do that, and it feels so fucking good. I alternate strokes of my cock and fingers, making sure some part of her is always full of some part of me. She screams as she comes again, harder than the first time, so hard there's no way I can hold out this time. I explode inside her, coming like I haven't had sex in a year rather than an hour.

We land on the blanket in a sweaty mass of limbs, aftershocks rocking us as we try to recover our breath. After a long period of quiet, marked only by the sound of our heavy breathing, we begin to disentangle ourselves. I help her sit up, brush the hair back from her face and tilt her chin up so I can see her eyes. She's glowing. I'm not sure if it's me or the heat or a combination of both, but she looks lovelier than she ever has before.

I kiss her softly and help her up and out of her dress, which seems unnecessary after what we just did. I lead her toward the water, scooping her up into my arms to carry her over the rocky edge. I keep her close to me as we drop into the water.

Honey wraps her arms and legs around me and rests her head on my shoulder.

A sense of peace comes over me, the likes of which I haven't known in so long, I almost don't recognize it for what it is. I'm content in this moment. And then I remember I told her last night that I could give her only one more night. Just that quickly, my feeling of peaceful contentment is upended by my reality. I have nothing to offer her. I'm a shell of a man who powers through life with the goal of surviving each day. I can't condemn a sweet, beautiful woman like Honey to that kind of existence. She deserves so much more. But damned if I don't wish, for the first time since I lost Jordan, that I could be someone different for her.

But she's here with me now, and I vow to enjoy every minute I have left with her soft curves pressed up against me. And when I take her home, I'll kiss her good-bye and go on with my life. As much as that will hurt, it's the right thing to do. It's the *fair* thing to do.

She reaches up to run her fingers through the hair that covers the nape of my neck, and I'm filled with longing for what can never be.

Honey

What a lovely day this has been. The sun is setting in a fireball of oranges and reds as Blake drives us back to town. We spent hours in the water, drying in the sun, and making love. It was blissful and relaxing and a million other things I don't dare allow myself to think about. I don't want it to end. I'd offer to make him dinner, but I don't want to overstep his boundaries. If I push for more than he's able to give, he'll run away. I don't want him to run away. I want him to keep coming back, but only if that's what he wants, too. So I bite back the urge to suggest more.

We pull up to my house far too soon, long before I'm ready to say good-bye.

My heart surges with excitement when he gets out to walk me in. But my excitement fades when he stops at the door and draws me into his arms. "Thank you for a fantastic weekend."

With my mouth suddenly dry, I force myself to smile up at him. "Thank *you* for not turning me down the other night."

"Even a machine would be a fool to say no to you," he says with that small grin I've become so fond of.

I hate that he sees himself that way. If anything, he feels *too* much and he loves *too* hard if he still feels the loss of Jordan as intensely as he did when it first happened.

Then he kisses my forehead and breaks my heart. It's over. I got exactly what I wanted from him—more soul-shattering orgasms than I ever could've hoped for. But that's all it's ever going to be, and I have to find a way to make peace with that.

I force my arms to drop from around his waist and take a step back out of pure self-preservation. "I had a really nice time."

"Me, too." He cuffs my chin playfully. "Take care of yourself, Honeycomb."

The nickname makes me want to sob for what could've been. My hands are shaking when I try to get the key in the door.

He takes it from me and does it for me. He steps back to let me go in. "Honey—"

I place my hand on his chest. "Don't say it, Blake. I'm okay. I promise."

Looking down, he nods, but I notice the tension is back in his jaw. "I'll see you around, darlin'."

"Yes," I say, forcing a cheerful tone. "You will." I close the door and slide down the back of it, dropping my head into my hands as a sob erupts from my chest. God, I'm such a fool! Lauren warned me against this very scenario, and here I am, crying my heart out for a man I knew could never be mine.

It was so good with him, so easy and familiar, yet new and exciting, too. How often do you find all that in one man? For me, never. And if only it had just been the sex that was amazing I could've moved on from that without feeling crushed. But the fact that *everything* with him was amazing is going to take some time to get past.

I felt a real connection to him and not just in bed. Our shared history, friends, upbringing, roots... All of it combined to bring a sense of familiarity to what might've otherwise been an awkward encounter.

I'm devastated to realize it'll never be more than one perfect weekend.

It's completely dark by the time I drag myself off the floor and into the shower, where I stay for so long, the hot water runs out. My body is sore and tired, and my head is aching almost as badly as my heart. I wrap a towel around my body, go into the kitchen to find some pain relievers in the closet where Gran always kept the medicine and nearly jump out of my skin when I find Lauren sitting at the kitchen table.

"What the hell, Lo? You scared the crap out of me."

"Likewise. I've been trying to call you all day, and when you didn't answer, I came to check on you and heard you crying in the shower. What's that about?"

"Nothing." I grab the pill bottle from the cabinet and wrestle with the cap.

Lauren comes up behind me, takes the bottle from me, opens it and drops two pills into my hand. Then she fills a glass with water and hands it to me. "Don't tell me it's nothing. I haven't seen you cry since Gran died."

I can hide from some people. Lauren isn't one of those people.

"Blake just left."

"Wait... He just left as in *today* he just left?"

Nodding, I wash the pills down with the cool water.

Lauren takes me by the arm and leads me to the kitchen chair she abandoned. I sit because that's easier than fighting her. She sits next to me. "Speak."

"He came over after the party last night. He said..." Why did this hurt so fucking badly? "He said he wanted one more night. Today, he asked me to go out to Jordan's grandparents' place. Did you know he bought it?"

"I hadn't heard that."

"He's restoring it and bringing it back to life. We went swimming and..." I blow out a deep breath that does nothing to soothe the ache that has overtaken me. I hope the pills help, but I suspect they can't fix this kind of pain. "He brought me home, and that's that."

"What did he say when he brought you home?"

"That it'd been fun." My voice breaks, and my eyes fill with tears that I angrily wipe away when they spill down my cheeks. "It *was* fun. I have no idea why I'm such a mess."

"Because you want more."

I shake my head. "I know that's not possible."

"Doesn't mean you don't wish it was."

And there she struck at the heart of the issue. I wish it *was* possible to take this amazing weekend and build upon it, to see what would've happened next, to at least *try* to make something with him. Suddenly, I'm sobbing again, emotionally wrecked by the disappointment, even if I know I'm being ridiculous.

"I was afraid of this," Lauren says when she wraps her arms around me.

"You tried to warn me. Hell, I warned myself, but I still got sucked in."

She grabs a paper napkin from Gran's wicker basket on the table and wipes my face and then holds it up for me to blow my nose. I'm reminded of the many times Gran did that for me, and it suddenly occurs to me all over again how alone in the world I really am. For two blissful nights, Blake made me feel less alone, and I think I did the same for him. "Maybe, when he has some time to think about it..."

"Don't," Lauren says. "Don't allow yourself to hope for that. We both know how he is." She's very businesslike as she wipes my face with a clean napkin and refills my water glass. "We're going to get you through this and move on. What would Gran say?"

I smile wanly. "That there's no sense crying over spilt milk." She was forever telling us that when we were girls.

"Exactly. She knew what she was talking about. You're her girl and every bit as tough as she was. Don't you ever forget it."

"I don't feel very tough right now."

"You'll get your mojo back in a day or two, and just think, now you know what it's like to have great sex."

She means that to be comforting, but all it does is remind me of what I'll never have again.

"You want me to sleep over?"

"You have to be in early for your flower delivery."

"I can get someone to do it for me."

"I'm fine, Lo. I swear. Just a momentary moment of madness." That sums up my current state of mind and describes the incredible weekend with Blake. "I've gotten through worse, right?" For a short time after Gran died, I wasn't sure I could go on without her. Thanks to Lauren and Julie and my other friends, I managed to drag myself out of that abyss. It didn't happen overnight, though.

"You certainly have. Call me if you need me? Even if it's the middle of the night?"

"I will." We both know I never will, but I tell her what she needs to hear. I pride myself on my independence and my resilience. The shadow of rejection has colored my entire life, so this feeling is nothing new.

I walk Lauren to the door and hug her. "Love you forever," I whisper. We've been saying that to each other since we met as first-graders and formed an instant bond.

"Love you forever." She hugs me tight, kisses my cheek and takes her leave. I stay at the door and watch until she's safely in her car. Then I shut off the porch light and lock the door. I go into my room to change out of my towel dress into lightweight pajamas.

I convince myself I'm feeling better until I get into bed and am assaulted by the scent of Blake's cologne on my pillow. I lose it all over again, sobbing like the heartbroken fool that I am.

Hugging the pillow to my chest, I take deep breaths of the scent, committing it to memory. I never want to forget one minute of the time I spent with him. It was the best time I've ever spent with any man, and it will be a long time, if ever, before I get over my weekend with Blake Dempsey.

CHAPTER NINE

Blake

The machine is back in business the Monday morning after the beautiful weekend with Honey. For a whole week afterward, I power through the way I always do, trying not to think about her or how much I miss her or what might've been with her. I can't believe it's possible to spend two nights with a woman and never want to leave, but that's just how it is. If I didn't know for sure I'd fuck it up somehow, I'd go back. But it's better for me—and certainly for her—if I stay away. So that's what I've done. I've stayed away, even if it has about killed what's left of me.

My company is building a shopping center outside of town, and I'm in the thick of it all day, every day with my men. We move mountains, doing the work of two days in one. As I head for my after-work beer, I'm completely exhausted at the end of the second Monday after my weekend with Honey.

My usual watering hole looks different to me now. Everything looks different post-Honey. I take my usual seat at the far left-hand side of the bar, and Jimmy brings me my usual bottle of Bud. Same thing, different day. Until Honey Carmichael came strolling in here that Friday night, my routine hadn't changed in longer than I can remember. And now all I can think of is her. Soft skin, sweet taste, hard nipples, tight pussy... *Fuck*, I'm suddenly hard as a rock for more of her.

I hate my own rigid rules more than I can say. I down that first beer and signal for another, noting Jimmy's surprise. I never, ever have more than one beer after work. I don't drink more than one beer and drive. Ever. That's one of the other nonnegotiable rules of my life after the accident. I never again want to be responsible for someone else getting hurt, or worse, because of me. They said it wasn't my fault. Fuck them. I was driving her, and she was killed. Of course it was my fault.

The second beer goes down easier than the first. I signal for a third and ask for a shot of Jameson to go with it.

"Y'all right, Blake?" Jimmy asks when he puts the beer and shot in front of me.

I push a twenty across the bar. "Never better." I want more of her so badly, I burn from the longing. As if it has a mind all its own, my cock refuses to be deterred and takes up all the space in my jeans. I'd find that funny if I didn't feel so shitty. I've got stuff to do tonight. Invoicing and estimates and paperwork that never ends, but I can't be bothered with any of it.

The last time I felt this bad... *Fuck*. I need another beer, and I need it now.

Honey

Eight days after the last time I saw Blake, I'm getting into bed after a long and trying day at the studio when the house phone rings. I almost don't bother to get it, because anyone who knows me well would call my cell. But cell service in Marfa can be spotty, so maybe my cell isn't working.

I go into the living room to grab the extension next to Gran's recliner. Yes, even ten years after she died, it's still her chair. "Hello?"

"Is this Honey Carmichael?" a man asks. In the background, I hear music and people talking.

"Yes, who's this?"

"It's Jimmy down at the bar. You came in here the other night and left with Blake. Right?"

I swallow hard at the realization that people actually witnessed my blatant proposition and recognized me. I wish the floor would open up and swallow me whole. And what does this guy want? Some of what Blake got? The thought of that turns my stomach. "Y-yes," I say, because I can't exactly deny it. "Why?"

"He's here now and drinking a lot more than usual. I tried calling his friend Garrett, but couldn't reach him. Any chance you might be able to come get him?"

I'm shocked to hear that Blake is drinking like that. He never does that anymore. "Yes, of course. I'll be there in fifteen minutes. Don't let him leave."

"He's not going anywhere, sugar. Not on my watch."

"Thank you for calling. Thank you so much." My hands are shaking as I get dressed and shove my feet into flip-flops. I nearly forget keys in my haste to get out the door. Once in the car, I drive way too fast on my way to Blake's favorite bar, also known now as "the scene of the crime."

For a whole week after our momentous weekend, every muscle in my body felt the effects of the sexual marathon. Naturally, I had several more difficult shoots, the worst today with yet another set of twins who cried for most of the time I was with them. I could relate. I wanted to cry all day, too.

I left the studio with a splitting headache and plans to again soak in the tub before an early bedtime. You know what they say about plans... Here I am, racing into the dark to rescue Blake from himself. My mind is spinning about why he decided tonight was the night to deviate from his usual routine.

Was it because of me?

Who am I kidding? He probably hasn't given me a thought since he kissed me on the forehead and left me on my front porch. He did exactly what he and Lauren said he would do, and there was no reason whatsoever that I should feel so disappointed. It's just that when he came over that second night and spent nearly twenty-four hours with me, he sparked a kernel of hope.

Foolish hope. I've been taught many times in my life that hope can be a disappointing bitch. Take when Gran rallied after chemo and radiation treatments. I began to hope that she might beat the cancer, but a month later, she was dead, along with my hope.

After that crushing loss, I learned to be careful about what I allow myself to hope for. Hoping that Blake Dempsey might suddenly decide he wants more from a woman, and that woman is going to be me, is so ridiculous that I find myself laughing hysterically. And then I'm crying just as hysterically. I hate that I've allowed myself to become so undone over what was supposed to be a one-night stand.

In truth, I'm nothing like the ballsy gal who blatantly propositioned Blake in a bar that Friday night. I'm actually much more like the soft-centered blubbering mess I am right now. I wish I was more like the ballsy girl, but Lauren pumped me up to the point that I actually believed I could *be* her.

It's not fair to blame Lauren. We were equally culpable in formulating the plan that worked exactly the way we hoped it would. It isn't her fault—or mine—that it worked a little *too* well.

I pull off the highway and into the dirt parking lot outside the bar. The weekend before last feels like a million years ago as I walk into the dark dankness that instantly takes me back to the high of my success that first night with Blake. Soaring highs lead to crushing lows. That's the lesson learned here. And judging by the condition I find Blake in, I might not be the only one suffering from the post-one-night-stand-that-turned-into-two-nights blues.

He's hunched over the bar with a row of empty beer bottles and shot glasses in front of him.

Jimmy, the bartender, nods to me as I approach Blake. I'm not sure if I should touch him or talk to him or what, but as I slide onto the stool next to his, I can't resist the need to touch him.

When my hand lands on his shoulder, he startles and swiftly looks over at me, his eyes lighting up with pleasure that quickly fades to misery so deep and so pervasive, I feel the ache of it in my bones.

"What're you doing here?" he asks, his words slurring.

"Jimmy called me. He thought you might need a ride home."

"Why you?"

"He saw us together the other night."

"You shouldn't be here, Honey. It's not the kind of place for a woman like you."

I want to ask him what kind of woman I am, but this isn't the time for questions. "Let me give you a ride home."

"Don't wanna go home. Nothing there. At least here I can get another round." He signals to Jimmy, who ignores him.

"I'll be there," I say before I can begin to contemplate what I'm offering or whether it's a good idea.

"You will?" The hopeful sound behind those two words travels straight to my heart, which is now, officially, overcommitted to him and this situation.

"Yeah, I will."

"You won't leave?"

I bite my bottom lip to keep from sobbing at the pain and loneliness I see in his eyes. "I won't leave."

"You promise?"

He's killing me here, one short sentence at a time. "I promise."

I take hold of his hand and give a gentle tug, urging him to come with me. I glance at Jimmy, who gestures for us to go on ahead. Blake's a regular, and he's good for what he owes. I smile gratefully at Jimmy and wrap my arm around Blake's wide back to escort him out of the bar.

Once again, everyone watches us as we make the slow, staggering journey to the door. I'm thankful for the small favor that Blake can actually walk. A few more boilermakers, and someone would've had to carry him out of here.

Texas heat hits us square in the face when we push through the door to the parking lot. Though he swerves a couple of times, he's generally cooperative in letting me steer him toward my car. The next challenge arises when I try to squeeze his six-foot-three-inch frame into my tiny car. I'm sure to outside observers, our struggle would be considered comical, but by the time I finally get him belted in, I'm sweating profusely.

During the drive to his house in town, he keeps his head back and his eyes closed while I try to remember to breathe while reliving his plea for me to stay with him. He doesn't want to be alone. My heart does a happy little dance at realizing he needs me. Despite that platonic kiss on the forehead, he's not done with me.

Hope soars within me like a phoenix rising from the ashes. Did I mention that I tend toward the dramatic when the occasion calls for it?

As I pull into the driveway at Blake's house, I'm assailed by the memories of what happened here that first night, heating me up for a whole other reason. I reach over to unbuckle his seat belt and go around the car to help him out.

He's dead asleep.

I shake his shoulder. "Blake. Come on. We're at your house. Wake up."

He doesn't move.

What the hell do I do now? I can't leave him out here all night to roast in this unrelenting heat. After a second to consider my options, I decide to plug his nose and force him awake. He comes to, sputtering and swearing, his eyes widening with surprise when he sees me standing over him.

"Honeydew... What're you doing here?"

He doesn't remember me picking him up at the bar? "Just helping you get home safe." I take his hand and help him from the car. When he slings his arm around my shoulder, he almost takes us both down, but I lock my knees and keep us from tipping over and then reach behind him to shut the car door.

Our stagger to the front door resembles a badly done three-legged race. "What's the code?" I ask when I see there's a keypad where the lock should be.

"Six, six, two, two," he whispers in the second before his lips descend upon my neck, almost making me forget the code he just gave me. I have to punch it in twice before the door finally swings open and we almost fall once again.

He begins to laugh, and I realize that it's been years since I've heard him laugh like that, as if he hasn't a care in the world. Maybe getting good and drunk was just what he needed.

"Let's get you to bed."

"Only if you're coming with me," he says in a low suggestive tone that has my girl parts standing up to cheer. *Yes, yes, yes*, they shout while my better judgment urges caution. Fuck my better judgment.

With my hands on his hips, I steer him toward his bedroom, intending to drop him on the bed and move to the sofa to keep my promise—and my distance. He has other ideas, however, and hooks his arm around my waist, all but dragging me with him to the bathroom. "Need a shower."

Not that he gives me much choice, but we end up in the bathroom with him tugging on the button to his jeans and clumsily ripping them off, which is a great way to find out he didn't wear underwear to work. I try not to look, but I'm only human and I'm totally besotted with The Cock that stands up tall and proud. Is it my imagination or is it leaning in my direction? Definitely not my imagination.

Blake leans in to turn on the water and tugs on my hand.

I fight back. I don't need a shower. I need a stiff drink and distance. Distance would be great right about now. "Let go! Take your shower."

"Need you," he mumbles.

Ah fuck, why'd he have to say that? While my brain asks *why*, my girl parts shout *yes, yes, YES! We are needed! Get your ass in that shower!* As I pull off my clothes, I suspect I'm going to regret this. In fact, I know I'm going to regret it, but I do it anyway. I step naked into the shower with the hottest man I've ever known—and his Cock with a capital C. His hands are all over me, touching, stroking, caressing, while his lips devour.

I'm immediately overwhelmed, with all my senses fully engaged and my defenses shattered by his touch as much as his obvious desire for me. The man who could barely stand when leaving the bar recovers his mojo in the shower. His hands cup my ass, and he lifts me up, pressing me back against the tile wall.

I gasp from the chill of the tile and the almost-painful stretch as he presses his way into me. How can this be happening when he's so drunk, he could hardly function half an hour ago?

He's all power and no finesse this time around, driving into me relentlessly, making me forget all about my resolve and the distance I intended to keep between us. Hell, he makes me forget *my own name.* Even when he's drunk and disorderly, it's so damned good with him. My fingers dig into his dense shoulder muscles as I hold on for dear life. I'm hanging in there until he starts talking and ruins me.

"Ahhh, Honey, God, your pussy is the sweetest I've ever had, the tightest, hottest Honeypot. Always loved you, since we were little kids, loved you. Honey... God, Honey." And then he's coming, and I'm trying not to bawl my head off from the things he's saying to me, things I've never suspected he felt, not once in all the years I've known him.

I want to tell him I love him, too. Of course I do. He's been a part of my life for as long as I can remember, and after being with him this way, he's wedged so far under my skin—literally and figuratively—I'll never get him out. I don't want him out. As I tighten my legs around his hips and move on his still-hard cock, I want him in, in, *in.*

I fist a handful of his hair and drag him into another heated kiss. I can taste the beer and the whiskey on his breath as his whiskers abrade the skin on my face. I don't care about any of that. All I want is more of the amazing way he makes me soar, body and soul. I've never flown as high as I do with him, and I'm becoming addicted to the way I feel when I'm in his arms.

He fucks me hard against the wall, so hard that my back will be bruised tomorrow. I don't care. I want more. I want everything. He fucks me until the water runs cold and shocks me when he shuts it off and hugs me tight against him to carry me from the shower to his bed. If you'd asked me half an hour ago to bet if he was capable of that feat, I'd have lost the wager.

We fall wet onto his bed, and he picks right up where we left off in the shower, his big cock surging into me over and over again, so hard and so fast I can't catch my breath before he's pressed deep into me again. This is insanity, and I never want it to end. The idea that every day and night could be like this for the rest of our lives is the most exciting thing I can imagine for myself—and him.

"I want you here," he growls in my ear, the press of his finger against my anus leaving no doubt as to what he wants. Though I can't imagine taking him there, I can't find the words to deny him. "Say yes. Tell me I can."

"Yes, Blake. I want you. I want you every way I can have you."

He withdraws from me suddenly and knocks the lamp off the bedside table in his haste to open the drawer where he keeps the lube. Somehow the lamp doesn't break, and the bulb glows from its new spot on the floor. There's just enough light for me to see the way his hands tremble as he lubricates the monster he plans to stick in my ass.

Maybe this isn't such a good idea. I begin to inch away from him, but he grabs my ankle and pulls me back. "Don't leave me, Honey. Please don't leave me. Need you."

Hearing this man who is known for being an emotionless machine profess his need for me is humbling, to say the least. My heart, soul and body are his to do with as he pleases.

"I love you, Honey. I'd never hurt you."

I brush back the hair that's fallen over his forehead. "I know. I love you, too."

The sweet smile that stretches across his face has my heart dancing once again. We're doing this, we're actually doing it. Blake Dempsey and Honey Carmichael are together. We're going to make a go of it, and I couldn't be happier. In fact, I don't think I've ever been happier about anything than I am about being with him and knowing that this time I get to keep him.

My celebration is interrupted by the intense pressure of him pushing his way into a place where no one else has ever been, and I quickly discover why—it hurts like a motherfucker. I can't do it. There's no way.

I'm about to tell him to stop when he presses his thumb against my clit and effectively splits my attention between back and front, which is now being coaxed toward an orgasm of potentially epic proportions. I don't know how he does it when he's had so much to drink, but he enters my ass slowly but surely, and at some point it stops hurting so badly I feel like I'm going to pass out. I wouldn't say it feels good—not by a long shot—but I no longer want to die from the pain.

A heated sensation is emanating in waves from my core and building on itself until it's all I can think about.

"Yeah, darlin'," he says in a low guttural voice that turns me on more than I already am—if that's even possible. "That's the way. Let me into that tight, hot ass. Hottest ass in town. Every guy in town wants to be me right now."

He rocks and rolls and pushes and shoves until that giant cock is fully seated in my ass, and then he presses again on my clit, and I ignite, coming so hard that I bite my tongue and taste blood in my mouth. I'm transported right out of this body, this room, this universe to a place I've never been before. I've never been anywhere even remotely like this place he takes me, and when I come back to myself, I discover he's fucking my ass, hard and fast, and I'm lifting my hips to encourage every deep stroke.

I did it—or I should say I'm doing it. I'm taking The Cock in my ass, and nothing has ever felt so amazing. In the back of my mind is the niggling thought that I won't be able to sit for a week, but who cares about that when another enormous orgasm rocks me, and him, too, if his sharp cry is any indication. He's so deep inside me that I can feel him in my belly. I feel the heat of his release and the ridges of his cock.

"Fuck," he cries as another wave of pleasure has him trembling on top of me.

This is, without a doubt, the most intense thing I've ever experienced, and I feel closer to him in this moment than I ever have to any human being, even Gran. I'm sobbing from the painful pleasure that consumes me. And when it's over, he collapses on top of me, his cock twitching and pulsing in my ass and his sweat mingling with mine.

He's breathing hard, but so am I. The weight of his body pins me to the mattress, but I don't mind. He loves me. He's wanted me for as long as he's known me. We're together now. Everything is working out the way the universe intended, and neither of us will ever be lonely again.

A low grunt precedes his first attempt to withdraw from me. I cry out from the pain of it. Who knew it would hurt as bad coming out as it did going in? Tears roll down my face from the tug of his cock against my sensitive flesh. It hurts like fucking hell. The head finally pops free, and I can breathe again as the tears flow freely.

He lands flat on his chest on the pillow next to me and passes out.

I stare up at the oddly lit ceiling thanks to the lamp on the floor. My body is on fire, and my heart is trying to catch up with what just happened. When my head finally stops spinning, I sit up and immediately regret moving and sitting. Oh my God... What've I done? I limp to the shower and pray the hot water heater has refilled in the last twenty minutes. I give thanks and praise to the god of hot water when I step into the shower and turn my back toward the spray. I look down and see the pink tinge to the water and realize I'm bleeding. Not badly, but a little. I suppose that's to be expected in light of what just happened.

It wasn't as bad as I'd thought it would be. At first it was pretty painful, but it got better, and he was careful with me. I'd do it again, I decide, not right away, but we've got all the time in the world to try new things, and I want to try everything with him.

I wash up and wince when the soap stings abused flesh. The hot water doesn't last long, and I get out to dry off. Back in the bedroom, I return the lamp to the bedside table and put the cap on the tube of lubricant before I put it back in the drawer, where there is also a box of extra-large condoms. I wonder why he has that stuff in there if he never brings women here. I'll ask him about that in the morning.

For now, I'm content to crawl into bed with him, to snuggle up to his warm body, to breathe in his appealing scent, even if the hint of whiskey in the air reminds me of how he spent his evening.

It's okay. He works hard and everyone has the right to blow off some steam every now and then. As long as no one gets hurt, why would it bother me if Blake did that once in a while? It wouldn't.

Nothing will bother me as long as he loves me and I love him. We can get through anything together.

Resting my hand flat on his back, I take that thought to sleep with me, a smile on my face and my heart at peace for the first time since I lost Gran.

CHAPTER TEN

Blake

A relentless pain in my brain wakes me from a sound sleep. Someone has driven an ice pick through my skull while I was sleeping. That's the only possible explanation for the agonizing pain. I try to move my head and discover that's the last fucking thing I should do, followed at a close second by opening my eyes to bright daylight.

Wait. What the fuck? I force my lids open again to find a mass of honey-colored hair on the other pillow. I know that hair. Why is she here? I let my gaze fall lower to her bare back and the two tiny dimples at the base of her spine. The sheet covers her ass, but the rest of her is a sight for my very sore eyes.

But what is she doing here? We're over. We both agreed it was for the best when I left her at her house the other night, even if I've regretted that stupid decision every second of every minute since. So why is she in my bed, and how did she get there?

I move painfully to my back and stare up at the ceiling, trying to remember what happened last night after work. I went to the bar, had a beer or maybe two. After that, my mind is blank. I don't recall anything beyond those first couple of beers. Jesus, when was the last time I drank myself to blackout?

Not since the months after Jordan died, when I did it so often, my family threatened to drag me to rehab. But like all things, time soothed my need to blot out the memories with alcohol. A relentless dedication to my work helped, too. I replaced the alcohol with my machinelike focus on staying as busy as I possibly could. It worked for me until I spent a weekend with Honey and got a taste of what I'd been missing out on.

And now here I am, drinking myself to blackout again. *Fuck.* The last thing in the world I want to do is go back to the black pit of despair that followed Jordan's death. I never want to sink that low again, which is why I've stayed far away from emotional entanglements with women. It's why I left Honey with that chaste kiss on the forehead the other night and ended this thing between us before it could get complicated.

So why is she here? What the hell happened last night? And why can't I remember a fucking thing?

Feeling like the proverbial kid in the candy store, I reach out to touch the soft silk of her hair, letting it slide through my fingers. Though I tell myself one touch and one touch only, I quickly go back for more while breathing in the sweet fresh scent of her hair.

She sighs in her sleep and then shocks me when she turns over and cuddles up to me, her soft breasts pressing against my side, her leg hitched over mine and her hand on my stomach, centimeters from the tip of my suddenly hard cock. Her breath flutters across my sensitive skin, and I hardly dare to breathe from wanting her so badly, I can taste it.

This can't happen. I thought she knew that. So why is she naked in my bed, and why am I filled with a sense of dread over what might've transpired during the lost night? I have so many questions and no answers.

Her leg slides up my leg, and her hand wanders south to wrap around my cock.

I gasp when she begins to stroke me in a slow, lazy rhythm. I'm filled with an almost painful yearning to begin each and every day exactly like this—with Honey pressed against me, her hand wrapped around my cock, her pussy hot and moist against my leg. That would be my idea of heaven.

The word heaven stops me short. That's where Jordan is, and she's there because of me. She never got to have any kind of life, so why should I allow myself the sweet pleasure and joy I could find with Honey? Why should I be allowed to let a beautiful woman like Honey love me and care for me when Jordan is gone forever and can never have any of that for herself? And what if I were to take this huge chance with Honey and something happened to her, too? I barely survived it the first time. There's no way in hell I'd ever survive it again.

I push aside the painful yearning and gently remove her hand from my cock, though that's the last fucking thing I want to do. Extricating myself from her soft skin and sweet fragrance, I sit up and take a minute for my pounding head to catch up.

"Are you okay?" she asks in a sexy, sleepy voice.

"Yeah. I'm fine."

"Do you want me to get you some painkillers?"

"No." The one word comes out more harshly than I intended, and I feel the loss of her body heat when she backs away from me. I'm a fucking asshole, and I hate myself for whatever series of events brought her to my bed last night. I only hope I didn't say or do anything that can't be undone.

"What're you doing here, Honey?"

After a long, *long* pause, she says, "Jimmy called me to pick you up."

"Oh. Okay. Thanks." That doesn't tell me one damned thing about why she's naked in my bed and stroking my cock like she has a right to.

Without looking back at her, I get up and go into the bathroom, intending to take a cold shower to wake me up and extinguish my raging hard-on. I stop short at the sight of our clothes, intermingled on the floor outside the shower. *Fuck, fuck, fuck!* Feeling more desperate by the second to fill in the missing gaps in my memory, I bend over to retrieve her thong, bra and dress, holding the items close to my chest for a brief moment before hanging them on the hook on the back of the door.

I feel sick, and not because of the beer still sloshing around in my gut. While the water warms up, I take a leak and desperately try to piece together the previous night. But like before, my memory ends with Jimmy, the bar, the beer, the... *Fuck*. Whiskey. That's why I can't remember anything.

Standing with my back to the water in the shower, I wonder if there's any hope at all that we didn't have sex. I glance down at my cock and note for the first time it's tinged with red. Is that... *Oh my God...* My heart begins to pound erratically and my hands don't want to work right as I quickly wash my body, including the dried blood on my cock. I made her *bleed?*

I'm going to be sick.

It takes a herculean effort to hold back the nausea that burns my throat. I sling a towel around my hips and reach for the door, noticing that her clothes are gone. Panic surges through me as I chase after her, running through the house and out to the driveway without a thought for decency or anything that doesn't include stopping her from leaving before we get the chance to talk.

She's pulling out of the driveway when I burst out of the house.

I chase her down the street, but either she doesn't see me or she ignores me. I suspect it's the latter. And more than that, I suspect I've done something awful to deserve her disdain and her hasty departure.

Honey

He doesn't remember. He doesn't remember. Oh my God, he doesn't remember.

The sentence cycles through my brain on repeat until I begin to fear I'll go mad if I have to think about it for one more second.

Tears slide down my cheeks, making it difficult to drive. Fortunately, I don't have far to go. Not only can I not see, sitting is excruciatingly painful. I choke on a sob. How can he not remember telling me he loves me and needs me and doesn't want to let me go?

How can he not remember the searing intimacy of what we did in his bed?

I'm going to die from the embarrassment as much as the heartbreak. Just when I thought I couldn't be a bigger fool than I'd already been with him, this happens to show me I've only begun to scratch the surface of my own stupidity.

Brushing away tears that refuse to quit, I'm not sure if I'm more hurt or angry. Hurt. Definitely hurt. The pain inside me reminds me far too much of how I felt when Gran died and I woke up the next day to realize I was all alone in the world. That's exactly how I felt this morning when it occurred to me that he had no memory of what transpired between us last night.

Now I feel like someone has run a spear through my chest, making it impossible to breathe or think or feel anything other than crushing pain. I arrive at home, and when it hurts to get out of the car, I decide to do something I never, ever, ever do. I'm canceling my appointments for the day to stay home and lick my wounds, which is just another reason to be furious with Blake. Now he's ruining my business along with my life. I make the necessary calls to cancel my day, apologize to my clients and reschedule them for later in a week that's already booked solid. It'll make for some long days, but at least I'm free today.

I draw a hot bath and dig out Lauren's box of Epsom salt. Gran swore Epsom was the cure for every ache and pain. I suspect the magic might not extend to broken hearts. Lowering myself into the steaming water, every muscle I have fights back, or at least that's how it seems to me.

Whimpering from the pain that radiates throughout my body, I begin to cry all over again, as if I haven't already dehydrated myself this morning.

All at once, someone is pounding on my door and yelling my name.

I'm frozen with indecision. He came after me. Surely that must mean something.

"No, Honey. It doesn't mean anything more than he feels bad that he doesn't remember last night. That's all it means."

I force myself to stay put, to not get out of the tub, to not answer the door even if I'm worried that my nosy neighbors will call the police. Let them. That'll be his problem, not mine.

He pounds on the door for at least ten minutes, yelling for me the whole time.

I close my eyes, cover my ears and pretend I can't hear him. Eventually, he'll go away—or be arrested. At this point, I'm not sure which outcome I prefer.

Finally, the racket stops, and the silence is almost as loud as the noise was.

I wait until the water goes cold before I drag myself out of the tub, put on my coziest robe and go to peek out the front window to make sure Blake is actually gone. There's no sign of him or his truck outside, and I'm gutted all over again.

"What did you expect? To find him sitting on your front stoop waiting you out? That only happens in bad movies." I make myself a cup of tea and take it to bed, where I plan to spend the rest of the day hiding from the world.

———

I'M SOUND ASLEEP LATER THAT AFTERNOON WHEN MY CELL PHONE rings, jarring me awake. I ignore it and turn over, intending to go back to sleep. It rings again.

I'm almost certain it has to be Blake, but I check the screen just the same and see Lauren's name along with a text from her that says 911. I take the call.

"Lo? What's wrong?"

"Thank goodness you answered, Honey! Where are you? There's been a water-main break on Highland, and the whole street is flooding. You need to get to the studio to save what you can. Honey? Do you hear me?"

"Yes, I hear you." I blast out of bed, ignoring my aches and pains, and pull on shorts, a bra and T-shirt. I jam my feet into sandals and run for the door, grabbing my keys on the way out. "I'm coming."

"Hurry, Honey."

As I drive the short distance into downtown Marfa, I try to think about what might be in the line of fire from the flooding. Mostly the hundreds of framed and matted photos I have available for sale in the studio. All the photos are backed up in the cloud, but I'd lose thousands of dollars in materials if they're ruined.

My most valuable equipment is stowed in a fireproof vault that I hope is also waterproof. Why can't I remember if it is? Surely I should know that. I turn onto Highland and immediately encounter water rushing toward me. At the far end of the street, I can see emergency vehicles and a geyser shooting water high into the air. Shop owners and business people are gathered on the sidewalks that line the street, keeping a close watch on the rising water.

For a second, I'm not sure if I should get out of the car and battle my way to the studio or if it would be safer to stay in the car. One of the local cops, a guy I grew up with, waves for me to go on ahead. Johnny wouldn't wave me through if it was dangerous, would he? I hope not.

I press the accelerator and hydroplane my way down Highland Avenue, pulling into the parking lot next to the studio and running for the back door, where the water is already ankle-deep. When I open the door, the water rushes into my pristine studio, and all I can think about is the entire weekend Lauren, Julie, Matt and I spent refinishing the wood floors. I'm no expert, but even I know that wood plus water isn't a good thing.

Determined to save what I can, I spring into action, grabbing armloads of matted photos and carrying them off the showroom floor to a table in the back room that's four feet above the water. If it gets that high, we're in really big trouble.

I splash through the water that continues to rush in through the front and back doors as I make numerous trips back and forth with armloads of stock photos. It's above my ankles and rising by the second. Why can't they shut it off or do something to make it stop? Grabbing up boxes of props that I use for my desert photos, I'm on the verge of panicking about the possibility of losing everything I've worked so hard for when Blake appears like an apparition at my back door.

He directs his men in a strong, authoritative voice, and they begin sandbagging my back door. "Go around to the front," he orders some of them. "Hurry."

Dumbstruck by the sight of him, I watch the muscles flex in his arms as he quickly builds a barrier of sand to keep the water out of my studio. As he works, he occasionally looks my way, his intense blue-eyed gaze slamming into me, putting me on notice that we have unfinished business.

"I'll be back," he says when they've built a wall of sandbags that slows the water to a trickle. "Be here."

He's gone before I can formulate a reply. And what exactly would I say to that anyway? I'm resigned to having one last conversation with him about what went on between us before we return to life as friends who've known each other since we were kids.

I can do that, or so I tell myself, trying not to think of the late-night encounter in his bed that tipped my world on its axis and filled me with relief and excitement and joy like I'd never known. It was all a tease. I get that now that I've had some time to accept that he doesn't remember anything that happened between us last night, even if I already know I'll never forget a second of it.

For one brief, shining moment, I had everything I've ever wanted in the palm of my hand, so close I could taste the sweetness of my future laid out before me with a strong but complicated man who loves me. Then it was snatched away ruthlessly, and no matter what he might have to say to me, I need to remember how badly that hurt.

I busy myself sorting through the photos that are now stacked in disorganized piles on my worktable. My gaze falls to one of my favorites, the famous Hotel Paisano, where James Dean, Rock Hudson and Elizabeth Taylor stayed during the making of the 1956 film *Giant*.

I've poured my heart and soul into my work because I didn't have anywhere else to direct my love since Gran died. My affection for Marfa, the town that rallied around an abandoned baby girl, shines through in every photo I've ever taken of the famous courthouse, the Marfa lights, the Chinati and the various art installations that make our town so unique.

I love this place and wouldn't want to live or work anywhere else, but now I'll have to worry about running into Blake in random places like the grocery store or post office, tearing the scab off the wound each time I come face-to-face with those cool blue eyes. I'm well aware it's a wound of my own making, beginning with the words "I want you to fuck me," but that doesn't make the wound any less painful.

"I'm sorry about that, Gran," I whisper to the silence that surrounds me in the studio. "I never should've propositioned him the way I did. You were right about the importance of being a respectable lady. But I don't regret anything that happened with him, except for the fact that it ended. I wish we could've had more time. I wish I could keep making him happy the way I did when we were together. More than anything, I wish he remembered what happened last night."

"Why don't you tell me?" he says from behind me.

I whirl around, shocked that he came back so soon, that he heard what I said, that he wants to know what happened.

He closes and locks the back door to my studio. "We're not leaving here until you fill in the blanks for me."

"It doesn't matter."

"I think it does. I think it matters a great deal."

"You were straight with me from the beginning. It's not your fault that I blew it up to be more than it was ever supposed to be."

"You're not the only one who did that."

"I'm not?"

He shakes his head. "Something happened last night. I know it did because I saw proof of it this morning."

I give him a questioning look, wondering what specifically he's referring to.

"Exhibit A was waking up naked with you. Exhibit B is the clothes I found on the floor of the bathroom—yours and mine mingled together in one pile. Exhibit C would be the dried blood on my cock that's had me spinning all day because I made you bleed, Honey. You have to tell me what I did, if I hurt you, if I—"

I can't bear the agony I see in his tortured expression. I go to him and place two fingers over his lips. "You took the last of my virginity, and I loved it. Mostly."

His eyes go wide with shock. "No..."

"It's okay, Blake. Really. You may not remember, but we both enjoyed it." I let my hand fall from his mouth. "I've loved the time we spent together, but I was aware of your rules going into it, and I respect them."

"Fuck my rules." His arm whips around my waist and pulls me in tight against him so quickly, I lose my breath as I crash into his chest. With his free hand, he tilts my face up to receive the most desperate, passionate kiss of my life. I can do nothing but hold on tight to his shirt and hope he keeps his arm around me so I don't become another puddle on the floor. "I want you, Honey," he says many heated minutes later. "I want more than just a weekend with you."

"How much more?" I fight to keep my foolish heart from jumping in before we have all the information.

"I'm not sure. I wish I could say that I'm capable of everything, but I honestly don't know if I am."

"You *are*, Blake." I flatten my hands on his chest and look up at him, hoping he can see that I'm putting my heart on the line. "You just have to give yourself permission to be happy. Can you do that?"

"I don't know. I can't remember what it felt like to be truly happy. It's been such a long time, years... And then a beautiful girl walked into a bar and turned my orderly world upside down." He tucks a strand of hair behind my ear and runs his fingertips over my cheek. The light caress makes me tremble.

"Did I do that?"

"You sure as hell did." He nuzzles my neck, and the scrape of his whiskers against my sensitive skin is an instant turn-on. Hell, everything he does turns me on. "Honey... There's one thing I have to know for certain."

"What's that?"

"You're really okay after last night? All I can think about is blood—"

I kiss the words off his lips. "I'm fine. I swear."

He releases a deep sigh that sounds like relief to me. "Let's get this water cleaned up, and then I want to take you on a proper date. Would that be all right?"

"Yes," I say, smiling up at him. "That would be all right."

CHAPTER ELEVEN

Honey

It takes hours to clean up the studio, even with the powerful pumps and vacuums Blake brings from his company. After we do everything we can to dry out the studio, we move to Lauren's flower shop, where we find my best friend in tears as she contends with the damage to her business.

I envelop her in a hug while Blake gets to work sucking up the ankle-deep water.

His friend Garrett joins us, and the four of us work together to clean up the mess.

Lauren orders food from the part of town that wasn't affected by the flood, and we devour the meal before going back to work. Outside, the sound of pumps running fills the air as other businesses clean up from the near-disaster.

Though I'm exhausted and aching from head to toe, I keep at it until most of the water is gone from Lo's shop.

Blake leaves us both with industrial-strength driers that will run overnight.

"I had no idea those things even existed," Lauren says when he drags the machine in from his truck.

"I bought them a couple of years ago, just in case," Blake says.

"Well, thank God for that," I say.

"No kidding," Lo adds. Her curly hair is piled on top of her head in its usual messy bun, and her brown eyes shine with unshed tears. "I can never thank you guys enough for helping me." She gives Garrett a shy smile. His dark hair and T-shirt are damp with sweat, but the grin he sends her way lights up his brown eyes.

"Happy to help," he says. "Any time."

I don't think he's as immune to her as she'd like to think, but I keep that thought to myself for now. There'll be plenty of time to dissect Garrett's potential interest with Lo after we get some sleep and have our emotions under control.

"Do they know what caused the main to break?" Garrett asks Blake.

"Haven't heard yet, but I got a call from the county that they needed help fixing it. I sent a team over there earlier. I'm waiting on a status report from Matt. The good news for you ladies is that they've managed to shut off the water, but that's bad news for everyone who lives nearby."

"You're one of the lucky ones," Garrett says. "Crisis is good for business."

"I'd never wish this on anyone, even if it is good for business."

I like his answer. I like it a lot. He feels for those of us who nearly lost everything, even if the flood will turn out to be profitable for him.

"Do you think it's safe to leave?" Lo crosses her arms around herself protectively as she inspects her disheveled shop. Like at my studio, we moved everything to higher ground, and it'll take her most of a day to put things back where they belong after the shop dries out.

"I'll stay for a little while longer if you want to be sure," Garrett offers.

She visibly brightens. "You will? Really?"

"Sure. I don't have anything going on tonight. It's no problem."

I can see she's fighting back tears that are due more to exhaustion than anything. It takes a lot to rattle my girl, but nearly losing her livelihood would bring anyone to tears.

"Call us if you need anything," Blake says, kissing Lo's forehead on the way out.

"Thank you so, so much, Blake. I don't know what I would've done without your help—and your stuff."

"My stuff is your stuff." He cuffs her chin. "Get some sleep."

"You, too."

Blake ushers me out the door ahead of him. "Leave your car here. I'll bring you back in the morning."

He hasn't said or done anything sexy except infer that we're spending the night together, but that's all it takes to make me forget that I'm tired and sore and emotionally drained. My nipples tighten, and my clit stands up to take notice of his hands on me as he helps me into his truck.

Before he can get away, I curl a hand around his neck and draw him in for a kiss. "Thank you. Those two little words seem so inadequate in light of what you did for me—and Lauren—today."

"Entirely my pleasure, Honeypot." He kisses me, softly and sweetly, as if he knows that's all I can handle right now. "You have to let me go if I'm going to drive you home."

"Oh," I say with a dopey grin. "Sorry."

Smiling back at me, he kisses me again. "I'm not sorry."

I watch him round the front of the truck, feeling happy and joyful despite the hellacious day we just put in. I get to go home with him at the end of it, and what could be better than that? Is it silly for me to be a teeny, tiny bit thankful to the flood that forced us to confront what's been happening between us?

Maybe, but I'm not sorry we've had this breakthrough or whatever you want to call it. I missed him terribly in the week we spent apart after our wonderful weekend, far more than I've ever missed any man I dated in the past. I carried the longing for him around with me like an ache that couldn't be soothed no matter how hard I tried.

He drives out of Lauren's parking lot and reaches for my hand, linking our fingers in a tight, possessive grip that thrills me. Blake

Dempsey wants to possess me. I can't think of anything better than that.

At my house, he tells me to wait for him and comes around to help me out of the truck. Normally, I don't require help, but I'm so tired, I happily accept it. Plus, it's another opportunity to have his arms around me. Call me a shameless opportunist, but I love being in his arms.

He keeps up the TLC theme when we get inside, steering me directly to the bathroom where he draws a hot bath and helps me out of my clothes.

I hold out a hand to him. "Come in with me."

"Love to." He keeps his gaze trained on me as he pulls the T-shirt over his head, revealing the extraordinary chest that's been the source of my fantasies since our first night together, and drops his shorts to reveal he was commando all day. I lick my lips and look up to see the fire in his eyes.

"Make room for me."

I scoot forward while he gets in and then relax against his chest.

He wraps his arms around me, and I sigh with pleasure. "Can I have a rain check on that date you promised me?" I ask.

"Absolutely. I'm toast after this crazy day."

"Me, too."

"Honey... I'm really sorry about what happened last night. I just keep thinking about what you said we did, and how ashamed I am about that happening when I was drunk. I never should've touched you, let alone... *That*. I feel like a monster."

I reach back to caress his face. "I knew you were drunk. I wish you remembered, but we were both at fault."

"I never drink like that. Or I haven't in years anyway. Won't happen again. I promise."

"Is it okay for me to ask... What brought it on this time?"

"It's okay for you to ask, and if you must know, *you* brought it on."

"*Me?* What did I have to do with you getting roaring drunk?"

"Everything," he says with a sigh. "I've thought about you constantly since that weekend we had together, and I wanted more but didn't know how to go about asking for it. I told you it would just be those two nights, and I wanted to be fair to you, so I stayed away, and that about killed me. I hit the bottle last night because I needed some relief from the longing."

His confession makes me sad for him and happy for both of us at the same time. "I missed you every day that you stayed away."

"You did? Really?"

"Really. I thought about you and us and the amazing sex we'd had nonstop."

"The sex was pretty damned amazing, but that was only part of it."

With my head resting on his shoulder, I look up at him. "What was the other part?"

"You, Honey. *You* were the most important part. I felt so... I don't know... calm when you were around. Peaceful. I mean, not all the time." He waggles his brows to convey his meaning. "But most of the time, I was calm. I'm not explaining this well at all."

"You're doing a great job of explaining exactly how I felt, too. Since Gran died, I've felt sort of lost and alone, and for a short time when we were together, I didn't feel quite so alone."

"Yes," he says with a sigh that sounds like relief. "That's it exactly." He tightens his arms around me and brushes his lips over my hair. "Earlier, when I thought I'd ruined any chance I ever had with you, it hurt like hell."

"I'm sorry you were hurting and that I didn't answer when you came to the door. I just needed some time to process everything."

"You needed some time to process that something big happened between us and I don't remember it."

"Something like that."

"What else happened besides what you've already told me?"

I can't say it. I can't tell him that we were throwing the L word around out of fear that he'll run away and never come back.

He nuzzles my neck and gently cups my breasts, running his thumbs over my nipples. "Tell me, Honeybee. I want to know. Fill in the blanks for me. Tell me everything."

I'm not sure if I can or should do that, but I resolve to try. "Jimmy called me because he remembered us leaving together that first night. He said you needed a ride home, so I drove out there."

Blake blows out a deep breath. "I hate the idea of you coming in there alone when I was too out of it to look out for you."

"No one bothered me."

"You were lucky—we both were. I shudder to think about any of the guys who hang out there touching you."

There's that possessive streak again—the one I shouldn't love as much as I do. "Anyway, I talked you into letting me drive you home, and you made me promise I would stay."

"And did you? Did you promise?"

"It seemed important to you, so I did." I cover his hands on my breasts with my hands, needing to touch him. "You fell asleep on the way home, and I had to plug your nose to wake you up."

He snorts out a laugh. "That's a dirty trick."

"It was the only way I could get you to wake up. I wrestled you inside, and you insisted we needed a shower. Then you dragged me in with you and somehow managed to recover enough to have shower sex that became bedroom sex when you carried me into your room."

"I wish I could remember that."

"I wish you could, too, especially the next part when you said you wanted me there, and begged me to let you. I couldn't say no to you because..."

"Why?" he asks, his tone urgent and desperate.

"You said you've loved me for as long as you've known me."

"Ahhh, Honey, *God*... I'm such an asshole."

"Why? Because it's not true?"

"No, because it *is* true, but that was no way to tell you so." He hugs me even tighter, so tight I have trouble breathing. "Let's get out of here." He releases me and gets out so he can help me. Wrapping a towel around me, he dries every inch of me and makes quick work of drying himself. Then he takes my hand and leads me to bed.

Blake turns the AC down to a cooler setting, and we snuggle in under the covers, meeting in the middle where he pulls me in tight against him. "I made you bleed, Honey," he whispers. "That's all I can think about."

"You didn't hurt me, not like you think you did. It did hurt, but I'm fine, and it was pretty great once it stopped hurting."

"Really? You liked it?"

"I liked it. It's not something I want to do all the time, but maybe on special occasions, I could be convinced."

I feel his lips curve against my forehead. "What would constitute a special occasion?"

"Our anniversary, your birthday, when you bring me flowers..."

"That's all I'd have to do to have this?" He squeezes my ass cheek. "Bring flowers?"

"They'd have to be really, *really* good flowers. Lo can hook you up."

"Good to know." He continues to caress my ass, sending tingles of awareness darting through my body. "I want to do it again when I'm stone-cold sober, so I can remember every detail."

"Get back to me about that in a couple of weeks."

"Did I like it?"

"You loved it. You said my ass was the tightest, hottest ass, and that every guy in Marfa wanted to be you right then."

He lets out a sound that's half growl, half groan. "It's so, *so* true, and I hate that it's all a blank to me. I'm going to need to fill in that blank or go crazy wondering what I missed."

When I feel the press of his cock against my belly, I realize the conversation has turned him on. "You want me to tell you all about it?"

"Mmm, yes, please do."

"After you begged me to let you, and I agreed—against my better judgment, I might add—you reached for the lube and knocked the lamp off the table. And by the way, if you never take women home with you, why is there lube and a box of extra-large condoms in your bedside table?"

"That's just where I keep them, but I swear to you, I've never had sex in that bed with anyone but you."

"I believe you. Anyway, you used your fingers and lubed me up, and then yourself, and then... I felt the most intense pressure."

He takes my hand and wraps it around his cock, moving it up and down in a slow, lazy rhythm. The moisture gathering at the tip provides lubrication, and he gets even harder. "Then what?"

"The head popped in, and I screamed. It hurt like hell."

"Ahh, darlin', I'm so sorry."

"You made it better by caressing my clit."

"Like this?" His fingers slide through the dampness between my legs to press against the knot of nerves.

"Yeah," I whisper breathlessly, "just like that. You made me come so hard when you were entering me there while doing that. And afterward, when I came back down from the incredible high, you were fucking me hard. You made me come again and you came, too, that time."

He groans, and his release floods my hand. "God, that was so hot, Honey. I want to record that whole story and listen to it over and over and over again."

"No sense recording it when we can just live it."

"Is that what you really want?"

"Is it what *you* want?"

"I asked first." As we banter, he continues to alternate small circles around my clit with deep strokes of his fingers inside me. He's got me continuously on the verge of release.

"I feel like we're back on that playground and you're pinching again."

His soft chuckle makes me smile. I love to hear him laugh, to know I'm making him happy and easing the terrible burden he's carried with him for so long now. Turning me onto my back, he kisses down the front of me, and I hold my breath, knowing where he's going and how amazing it'll feel.

He props my legs on his broad shoulders and replaces his fingers with his tongue. He's got me so primed that it doesn't take much to take me the rest of the way to a slow, lazy release that rolls through me like waves rather than explosions. It's no less satisfying than the explosions.

Blake stays with me through the last wave and then gathers the moisture on his fingers to gently rub my anus.

I gasp from the pleasure as much as the residual ache.

"I'm sorry I hurt you," he says. "It'll never happen again."

"I know. It's okay."

"Not okay."

"Come up here." I reach for him and draw him into my arms to kiss and hug and soothe him. "Nothing happened that I didn't want. Do you hear me?"

"Yeah," he says gruffly. "I hear you, but I still wish it hadn't happened the way it did."

"Let's move on. Gran always said it's better to look forward than backward. We can't change the past. We can only live for right now."

"Your Gran was a wise lady."

"She was the best person I ever knew. I wish I was more like her."

"Why would you say that? You're perfect the way you are."

"The girl she thought she raised never would've walked into a bar and asked a man to fuck her."

"That was the coolest, ballsiest, most awesome thing that's ever happened in my entire life, so please don't turn it into something you feel you need to be ashamed of. I'd hate that."

"Will you do me a favor?"

"Anything."

"If we ever have grandchildren together, will you promise me you'll never tell them the story of how we got together?"

He stares at me for a long moment, during which I have no idea what he's thinking—or if I've gone too far down the road too quickly. "You see us having grandchildren together?"

I rest my hand on his handsome face and stare into the blue eyes that have utterly captivated me. "I see us having everything together."

CHAPTER TWELVE

Blake

I'd forgotten how it feels to be really, truly happy. I'd forgotten what it's like to have somewhere better to be at the end of every day than a bar where no one gives a shit about me—except Jimmy, apparently. Every night I get to come home to Honey, and every morning I wake up to her sweet face on the pillow next to me.

And in between getting home from work and waking up in the morning?

Whoa. Amazing. Just flat-out incredible. I'm not just talking about the sex, which is all those things. It's *her*. It's how I feel when I'm with her, like I've come home or something equally cheesy.

I'm incredibly happy, and the people around me are noticing, beginning with the guys I work with who've been busting my balls for whistling at work. I know, it's funny, and if it were one of them who suddenly started getting laid—and whistling—I'd be all over it the way they are.

Doesn't bother me. Not much bothers me these days.

My parents and siblings have also noticed that something has changed. They don't know what or *who*—yet—but they will, soon enough. We have a family reunion next weekend, and I'm planning to bring Honey to meet the aunts, uncles and cousins. She already knows my parents and siblings, but she hasn't met my nieces and nephews yet, and I'm looking forward to that.

I bet she'll be great with them, and they'll love her as much as I do.

You heard me right—I love her. Like I told her—once when I was drunk and again the next day—I've always loved her. It pains me to admit that I had a thing for Honey even when I was with Jordan. Not that it kept me from committing fully to Jordan. It didn't. I was all-in with her, but always, in the back of my mind, was Honey, unattainable, remote, out of reach until that night in the bar that I'll never forget.

I want you to fuck me.

Before that night, I never would've believed that six words could change a life, but they changed mine so profoundly, I almost can't remember what it was like before she said them. Truthfully, I don't want to remember what it was like to be lonely and bored and relentless in my efforts to work so hard that I didn't have time or energy to do anything else but eat and sleep and occasionally indulge in a meaningless screw.

I'm not proud of my drive-by relationships, especially the one I had years ago with Lauren when I was still reeling from the loss of Jordan. She was there for me, and I took the comfort anywhere I could find it. I've always been thankful that she doesn't hold it against me, and we're still friends. I'm especially thankful now that I'm in love with her best friend, who is snug against me on the sofa as we watch a chick flick that she was dying to see.

An hour in, I have no idea who's in the movie or what it's about. Why would I bother to care about that when I have her in my arms? I breathe in the fragrant scent of her hair and think about how I'm going to fuck her. She loves my creativity in bed, and I like to keep her guessing about what's on the menu on any given night. We go on amazing dates, like the night when we drove out of town so Honey could take pictures of the Marfa Magical Lights and then ate at the

Food Shark Museum of Electronic Wonders & Late Night Grilled Cheese Parlour, a local institution.

Life is good. I can't believe that I, Blake Dempsey, the emotionless machine of a man, is actually saying that, but it's true.

Knowing how easily I'm able to distract her, I let my fingers dip under the hem of one of her sexy-as-fuck tank tops that I swear she changes into after work so I'll be hard as a rock every damned night. If that's her strategy, it works, as does my strategy of distracting her with the drag of my fingertips over her taut belly.

I'm completely addicted to the softness of her skin. I love that she's lost her tan lines after a few more trips to the swimming hole for skinny-dipping, sunbathing and lovemaking.

When I bought the place, I figured I'd bring it back to life and then sell it at a profit. But now, I've begun to picture a life with Honey in the farmhouse that once belonged to Jordan's grandparents. I see a bunch of little blond kids running around, chickens and goats in the yard and maybe a horse or two in the barn. The more time Honey and I spend out there, the more clearly I see it. I have no idea what she sees in the future, but we have plenty of time to figure that out.

I continue to stroke her skin, working my way up to cup her breast. I love the way she pushes her ass against my cock, rubbing me shamelessly while she continues to watch the movie—or at least I think she's watching the movie. Pinching her nipple between my fingers, I give it a gentle tug.

"What're you up to back there?" she asks, sounding breathless and aroused, the way I love her best.

"Just watching the movie."

"You are not!"

I laugh at her indignant tone. "I am."

"What's it about?"

"Some chick who wants a dude and isn't smart enough to walk into a bar and ask him to fuck her to move things along."

She shakes with silent laughter. "Are you *ever* going to forget that?"

"Never, ever, ever, *ever*." I continue to tug on her nipple until it's hard and pointy and she's actively squirming. "You still watching the movie?"

"Depends."

"On what?"

"On what else is on the agenda for this evening."

"Darlin', you know what's on the agenda, but you really wanted to see this movie." I release her nipple and start to pull my hand away. "I'll leave you alone."

Her hand on top of mine stops my retreat. Thank goodness. The last fucking thing I want to do is stop touching her. She turns so she's on her back, looking up at me. "What would you rather do?"

"Absolutely anything that gets me inside of you." I love the way her cheeks flush and her eyes go wide when I say something like that. What I love even more is when she shocks the shit out of me by grabbing the hem of her tank and peeling it up and over her head and then shimmying out of her shorts and panties.

Wow, look at all that gorgeous honey-colored skin.

"Well?" she says with a saucy grin. Then she raises her arms over her head, offering herself to me. The trust I see in her eyes and in her expression humbles me.

"You're so beautiful, Honey. Every inch of you is beautiful."

"You make me feel beautiful."

I flatten my hand on her belly and watch the muscles flutter under my hand. She's so responsive, and her heart is wide open to me. I'm well aware that I have the power to hurt her. The thought of that kills me. I never want to hurt her. All I want is to make her as happy as she's made me.

She tugs on the button to my jeans and unzips me. "You're overdressed." Rather than go straight for my cock the way I expected her to, she drags her fingers over the hair that leads to my groin. I had no idea why that was called a happy trail until she touched me there, and now it makes perfect sense. Everything she does to me, every touch, caress, gesture and sexy, loving look she sends my way makes me happy.

"Take them off," she says of my jeans.

I wiggle my way out of them with her help.

"Sit up."

She seems to be enjoying telling me what to do, so I follow her orders. That pays off when she straddles my lap and brings the heat of her core down on my cock, tilting her hips back and forth and generally driving me nuts.

I reach around her to fill my hands with her supple ass cheeks, squeezing and shaping them as she drags her breasts over my chest. This is the sweetest sort of torture, and I love the leisurely pace, knowing we have all the time in the world to explore and bring each other pleasure. I'm her slave, and she knows it, the little vixen.

"Why are you smiling?" she asks, looking down at me from her perch on my lap.

"Because you're so sexy."

"You think so?" She's the hottest babe in town. Everyone knows that, except, apparently, her, but that hint of insecurity is just another thing to love about her.

I push my hard-as-a-rock cock against her pussy. "You really have to ask?"

She lifts herself up, high enough to press the tip of my cock into her wet heat, sinking down on me in slow increments that have me counting backward from one thousand as I try not to blow my load like an untested boy. The more we do this, the easier it is for her to take me, but we still go slowly at first, giving her body the time to stretch to accommodate me. I never want to hurt her or give her reason to avoid having sex with me.

She winces, and I grasp her ass cheeks to slow her down. "Take it easy, Honey Bunches. We're not in any rush."

"I hate when my body won't let you in."

I rub my thumb in circles on her clit while sucking her nipple into my mouth. The combination always helps to ease the way, and this time is no exception. "See?" I say as she sinks farther down on my shaft. "You can do it."

"Hmmmm."

"Tell me how it feels."

"Big," she says on a gasp. "Tight."

"Those are good words. Give me more." I pull her in closer to me and gain another inch.

"Hot, wet, thrilling."

"Is it? Thrilling?"

She takes my hand from her breast and lays it flat on her chest so I can feel the fast and frantic beat of her heart. "You tell me."

I can't breathe over the rush of emotion that catches me completely unprepared. Just when I think I can't feel any more, she surprises me. "I love you, Honey." I never get tired of telling her that or hearing her say it to me.

"Love you, too. I'm obsessed with you. It's not healthy to be so obsessed with a man."

"Yes, it is." I love that she's obsessed with me. I'm going to come so damned hard. "It's incredibly healthy as long as the person you're obsessed with is equally obsessed."

She finally takes all of me and throws her head back in complete surrender. It's the most exquisite thing I've ever seen. She is, quite simply, *mine. All* mine.

"Ride me, darlin'. Make me come."

Honey bites her bottom lip and begins to move, and fuck if it's not the most erotic thing I've ever seen. The drag of her pussy on my cock, the bounce of her breasts, the pulse that throbs in her throat and the flush that heats her cheeks are almost too much for me to take all at one time.

I reach down to where we're joined to make sure I'm not the only one who's going to explode. She doesn't disappoint me, and when she comes, the tight grip of her muscles on my cock is my undoing.

Honey collapses on top of me, and I wrap my arms around her, wanting to keep her close to me for a while longer. Who am I kidding? I want to keep her close to me forever.

"I can't believe you're still hard after that," she says after a long period of silence.

"It's your fault."

"How is it my fault?"

"He never gets tired of being inside you."

She shivers in my arms. "When you say things like that..."

"What?"

"I believe that it's really possible we're going to make this work."

"It is possible, and we *are* making it work. Already."

"Please don't change your mind."

"I'm not going to. I promise."

Honey

At first I'm not sure what woke me up. It's the middle of the night. Blake is asleep next to me, but he's restless. His legs are moving, and with the faint glow coming from the nightlight, I can see his hands are gripping the comforter in tight fists.

I lay my hand on his chest, and I'm shocked to discover he's drenched in sweat, and his heart is pounding under my palm. "Blake." I scoot closer to him and kiss his shoulder. "Babe."

He cries out like he's in agonizing pain.

Alarmed, I sit up and put my hand on his face. "Blake! Baby, wake up!"

He mutters something unintelligible and then whimpers.

I can't bear to see him hurting, even if he's hurting in his sleep. Leaning over him, I kiss his face and then his lips.

He comes to with a start, his eyes wild as they dart around the room.

"I'm right here, Blake. You're okay."

"I, um..." He scrubs a hand over his face and abruptly gets up to use the bathroom.

While I wait for him, I stare up at the ceiling, wondering what he was dreaming about and whether he'll tell me.

He's in the bathroom for quite some time, and when he slides back into bed, his skin is cool and his breathing back to normal. "Sorry to wake you."

"Please don't apologize. Do you want to tell me about it?"

"No, not really."

Stung by his sharp tone, I sink back into my pillow and literally bite my tongue to keep from pushing him. I already know that's the fastest way to shut him down, so I resolve to respect his boundaries and his privacy, even if I have a pretty good idea of what he was dreaming about.

We're quiet for a long time, so long that I suspect he's gone back to sleep. But then he breaks the silence. "I'm sorry. I don't mean to be short with you, Honeydew."

"It's okay."

"No, it isn't." He rolls over to face me and reaches for my hand, linking our fingers.

That's all it takes to put everything back on track, at least for me. "I have nightmares about the accident. I always have. It's one of the reasons I hardly ever spend the night with anyone." He squeezes my hand. "Until recently."

"I'm so sorry you have to relive it that way."

"It's ironic because I have no memory of the actual accident, but it plays out in living, breathing color in my dreams. I see the truck coming at us, and I know what's going to happen, but I can't do a thing to stop it."

It breaks my heart to know he still suffers so profoundly from something that happened nearly twelve years ago. While the rest of us found a way to go on after we lost Jordan, in many ways, Blake is still stuck at day one.

"I never know when the nightmare is going to come back. I'd understand if you didn't want to sleep with me."

"Nothing could make me not want to sleep with you. When the nightmare comes, we'll deal with it together. You're not alone anymore." I tug on his hand and urge him to come closer.

Sighing, he lays his head on my chest.

I wrap my arms around him. "Go back to sleep. I've got you."

"Honey..."

"I know." I kiss the top of his head and run my lips over the silk of his hair. "I love you, too."

CHAPTER THIRTEEN

Blake

Today's the day we make our debut to my family, and I'm nervous. Not about whether I want Honey with me, because I do. I want her with me every second of every day. No, I'm nervous because I know this will be as big of a deal to my family as it is to me. They haven't seen me with another woman since Jordan died. They'll understand the significance of me bringing a date to a family party, which is why I feel the need to warn Honey.

I bring coffee into the bathroom, where she's fussing over her hair, not that it needs anything extra to be beautiful. Putting the coffee on the vanity, I kiss her bare shoulder.

"I won't make us late," she says. "I promise."

"Take your time. They're not going anywhere. It'll go long into the night with a bonfire and s'mores and fireworks and more food than an army can eat in a month."

"Sounds wonderful," she says with a wistful sigh. "I've never been to a family reunion before."

The statement makes me ache for how alone she's been. "This'll be the first of many we'll go to together. My family will be your family."

In the mirror, I can see that my words have brought tears to her eyes. God, I love her. I love her so fucking much. I love her sweetness and her vulnerability as much as her effortless sexiness.

"I think I'm ready."

I take a step back to give her room to turn around.

"Do I look okay?"

She's wearing a simple yellow dress that offsets her light tan. "You look even more gorgeous than usual."

Resting a hand over her belly, she says, "I'm kinda nervous. I mean, I know your folks and your brothers and sisters, but going there together..."

"It means something."

She nods. "Exactly."

"True confession? I'm a little nervous, too, for the same reason."

"Oh," she says, her smile faltering ever so slightly.

"Not because I'm bringing you, but because I expect them to make a big deal out of it. I'm afraid that'll scare you off."

She flattens her hands on my chest and looks up at me, all sunshine and light and everything I need to be happy. "Nothing could scare me off."

"You say that now. Wait until you get a belly full of the Dempseys all at one time."

"I say that forever."

I release a deep breath and let the tension drain out of me. What do I care if this is a big deal to my family? As long as I have her there with me, it'll all be fine. "Let's get going."

Honey packs up the potato salad and cookies she made this morning and gathers the bunch of sunflowers from her Gran's garden that she cut for my mom, as well as her camera bag that she rarely leaves home without.

I help her carry it all out to my truck and get her settled before I walk around the front and get in the driver's side. We back out of her driveway, and she reaches for my hand, something that's become a habit I've grown used to. She holds my hand as we drive out of town to my aunt and uncle's ranch, where the party is being held.

When we arrive, I let go of her hand long enough to go around the truck to help her out, shouldering her bag of food as well as her camera bag. I grasp her hand again to walk across the wide expanse of brown lawn, around the sprawling ranch house that was a second home to me growing up, to the backyard, where a tent protects guests from the heat of the West Texas sun.

The pool is full of screaming kids, including my nieces and nephews. My eight-year-old nephew, Liam, lets out a shriek when he sees me. The next thing I know, he's racing across the yard to jump on me, wet bathing suit and all. I release Honey's hand so I won't drop the little monkey.

"Uncle Blake, are you gonna swim with us?"

"You bet, buddy. Just let me say hi to everyone, and then I'll be right there."

"'K." He looks past me to Honey. "Who's she?"

Smiling at the blunt question, I tell him, "That's my girlfriend, Honey. Can you say hi to her?"

"Hi, Honey. That's what my mom calls me."

"My Gran called me that so much that everyone started calling me Honey."

"That's cool." He begins to squiggle, wanting to get back to the pool.

I let him down, and he runs off. I look up to see my parents walking over to us, hand in hand as usual. They know I've been busy lately, but until right now, they haven't known why. Judging by the delighted expressions on their faces, my arrival with Honey is good news.

"Honey!" Mom says. "It's so nice to see you!"

"You, too, Mrs. Dempsey."

Mom hugs Honey. "Oh, please, call me Joan. We're all adults now."

I can see that Honey is touched by Mom's genuine pleasure in seeing us together. "Thank you, Joan."

"And I'm Mike," Dad says, giving her a hug and then giving me one.

His grip is extra tight, and when he lets me go, I notice his eyes are damp.

Right in that moment, I finally understand how difficult my years of grief have been on them, which disposes of the nerves I arrived with. They're thrilled to see me happy again.

Smiling widely, my mom gives me a kiss on the cheek and hooks her arm through mine. They escort us into the tent, where we're swarmed by aunts, uncles, cousins and family friends, including, I realize all at once, Jordan's parents.

My stomach drops to my feet, and I release Honey's hand. I'm not sure why I do that, but it doesn't feel right to hold hands with another woman in front of them.

They come over to greet me with hugs, smiling as they always do. Never once have they made me feel responsible for the loss that shattered us all. Rather, they've continued to treat me like a member of their family, and I've never been more humbled by that than I am right now.

Mrs. Pullman gives Honey a hug. "It's so nice to see you, Honey. It's been too long."

"Yes, it has." Honey returns her warm embrace, but I hear the emotion in her voice. She gets how hard this is for me, and I love her for that.

"It's so nice to see you both," Mr. Pullman says.

"And to see you smiling, Blake," Mrs. Pullman adds. "That's the nicest thing of all."

"Thank you," I say softly, humbled by their unwavering support of me, even when I feel I don't deserve it.

"I couldn't agree more," Mom says. "This calls for a celebration. Mike, let's get out that champagne we brought and toast to happy new beginnings."

I glance at Honey and notice her smile as well as the bright shine in her eyes.

My family loves Honey and me together, and so do Jordan's parents. I reach for Honey's hand and hold on tight to my love. Honey's Gran was right when she said we can't change the past. We can only live for the present, and my present is pretty damned sweet with her by my side.

Honey

At the end of our second month together, Blake talks me into taking a week off, and we drive ten hours to South Padre Island, south of Corpus Christi. I've never been here before and fall instantly in love with the beach, the palm trees and the relaxed vibe. It's here that I find out how much he loves to fish, and he patiently teaches me to enjoy it, too.

He planned the whole getaway, right down to the resort with the spa where he booked me a massage that I thoroughly enjoy.

I can't remember the last time I took a vacation of any kind, and it'll take a lot to top this one. We spend days in the sun, nights in bed and sleep in every morning before ordering room-service breakfast.

"I never want to go home," I tell him on our last morning.

"We can come back any time you want."

"Any time?"

"Any." He kisses me. "Time." He kisses me again and drops something onto my chest before he pulls back.

It's a small black velvet box. I stare at it like it's dynamite.

"Open it," he says, clearly amused by my reaction.

"I... What..."

"Open it, Honey-do list."

My hands are shaking so hard, I can barely get them to cooperate as I fumble the box open to reveal a stunning diamond solitaire. "Blake..." His name escapes from my lips on a long sigh. I did *not* see this coming. Not yet anyway.

He takes it from me and removes the ring from the box. "I love you, Honey Carmichael. I want to spend every day for the rest of my life the same way we've spent the last two months—together. We've known each other all our lives, so it's not like we're rushing into anything." He takes my left hand and kisses the back of it before sliding the ring onto my finger. "You brought me back to life with six little words in a bar, and now, I'm asking you to be my wife. Will you marry me, Honey?"

I'm completely blinded by tears and seem to have lost the ability to speak. All I can do is stare at the incredible ring he chose for me.

"Honey pot? You might want to say something here. I'm sort of dying."

"Yes, Blake, yes. I'll marry you. I love—"

I don't get to finish my sentence, because he's kissing me so fiercely. We roll across the bed and only stop when he's settled on top of me. He gazes down at me, his heart in his eyes. "Did you really say yes?"

"Did you really ask me to marry you?"

We both say, "*Yes*."

"Are you happy, Honey?"

"Do you really have to ask?" The question has become one of our favorite refrains, and he smiles in acknowledgment.

He cups my face and strokes my cheek with his thumb. "I never thought I could be this happy again."

Hearing him say he's happy is wonderful, but experiencing his happiness through frequent smiles, jokes and laughter is even more rewarding. "I brought a surprise for you, too," I tell him.

"Ohh, what is it?"

"Let me up, and I'll get it."

He kisses me and lets me out of bed.

I go into the closet to retrieve the item I brought from home, hoping we'd get the chance to re-create a significant moment in our relationship, this time when we're both sober. The light streaming in through the window reflects off my ring, and my heart gives a happy lurch. I can't wait to tell Lauren, Julie, Scarlett and everyone at home that we're engaged. I so wish I could tell my Gran, too, but I suspect she probably knows.

"Where'd you go?" he calls from the bedroom.

"Coming!" I try not to think about the last time we did this and how much it hurt. I suspect it'll be better this time when we're both aware of what's happening. I return to the bedroom and get back into bed.

"Where's this surprise I was promised?"

I open my hand to reveal the tube of lubricant I took from his bedside table. I watch with satisfaction as his eyes go dark with desire.

"Honey…"

"I don't like that I remember it and you don't. I thought maybe we could fix that."

"You… you want to?"

"If you do."

His eyes roll back in his head dramatically. "If I want to," he says on a snort. "Fucking hell, have you *met* me?"

"I've met you and I love you and I trust you and I'm going to marry you, and I want to have this memory that we both share."

He caresses my face in that tender way of his that tells me how much he loves me. "I'll never forgive myself for that night."

"I forgave you a long time ago. It's long past time you forgave yourself." I kiss him and press my breasts to his chest, a move that usually gets things moving right along. This time is no different. His arm bands around my back, keeping me right where he wants me for a devouring kiss.

"You're so amazing, Honey. I can't believe you were right here all this time."

"We weren't ready for this before now."

"No, I don't suppose we were. Now that I have you, I'm never letting you go."

"You'd better not." The very thought of it strikes terror in my heart. "I've been abandoned enough for one lifetime."

"That's not something you ever need to worry about again."

"So…" I take the cap off the lubricant. "Shall we have some fun?"

"Oh yes, darlin', we absolutely shall."

———

IT'S MUCH BETTER THE SECOND TIME, MAYBE BECAUSE MY PARTNER IS sober and aware in a way he wasn't the last time. That's not to say it's easy, because, hello, The Cock is never going to be easy to take there, but it's definitely better. He takes his time and puts all the focus on making it good for me, but I can tell by his exaggerated groans that it's good for him, too.

I'm on my knees with my head resting on my folded arms as he takes his own sweet time about it. He gives me a little and then retreats to do it all again, each time going deeper than the time before.

"Talk to me, Honey. Tell me how it feels."

"I'm expected to talk while you're doing that?" My voice sounds squeaky and higher in pitch than usual.

"Yeah," he says, sounding tense. "I can't see your face, so you have to tell me you're okay."

"I'm fine. You?"

"I'm about to explode, but other than that, all good."

I smile at his confession, and I love knowing he likes this so much. That makes the pain of his entry worth the inevitable pleasure we'll both take from this incredibly intimate act.

I lose all track of time and space and anything that doesn't involve him and what we're doing. I have no idea how long it takes for him to fully enter me, but once he does, I begin to focus more on the pleasure than the pain.

His fingers find my clit, which is hard and tingling with endless desire for this man who is going to be my husband.

I still can't believe he proposed. I'd had no idea that was coming so soon, and now that we have our future planned out, I can relax and enjoy every second we have together.

"Need to move, Honeybun," he says on a groan. "Gotta move."

Seeking purchase, I fist the sheet and grit my teeth, preparing myself. "Okay."

"Stop me if it's too much."

"I will."

I hear and feel the squirt of more lubricant before he begins to withdraw and then presses back into me while continuing to stroke my clit.

"Ah, Honey, God... I've never seen anything hotter than your sexy ass taking my cock."

I grunt out some sort of reply that's not really a word or anything he can understand, but he gets it. He knows I'd stop him if I didn't like it as much as he does. I push back against him, making him groan loudly, so I do it again and again until we're both moving and coming with shouts of pleasure that will wake the people next door to us if they're still sleeping.

My orgasm is so intense that I can't be bothered to care if we're disturbing our neighbors. I can't seem to tamp the keening cries that come from deep inside me. He's right there with me, pressing deep into me and heating me from the inside with his release.

We land on the bed in a sweaty pile of limbs. As he's still buried deep inside me, I feel every twitch and aftershock of his orgasm.

"Amazing," he whispers. "Just when I think it can't get any better than it already is, you blow my mind."

"You liked it?"

"You have to ask?"

I laugh softly at his predictable reply.

"I loved it," he says, "almost as much as I love you."

"I'll never get tired of hearing you say that."

"I'll never get tired of telling you." He holds me close for a good long time before he withdraws, slowly and carefully. "I hate to say it, but we need to hit the road."

"You know, we're both self-employed, and if we choose to take one more day for ourselves, no one can fire us."

"I do like the way you think, land of milk and Honey, but I've got an important meeting tomorrow with a new client, and I've done nothing to prepare."

The new nickname makes me giggle. "Oh, all right. If you're going to be all responsible about it."

He kisses the back of my shoulder and then runs his tongue over the shell of my ear. "I'll bring you right back here for our honeymoon. Oh, another name for my love. Honeymoon. I like that one."

My smile is so big I should worry about it breaking my face. We shower together and pack, and on the way out, I take a last look at the place where we got engaged, hoping we can get back here again sooner rather than later.

Blake holds the hand that now sports his ring as he drives his truck north toward Corpus Christi. We leave the windows open to breathe in the sea air as we travel along the peninsula. He's got the radio set to a country music station out of Corpus, and the music, fresh air and the knowledge that he's right there next to me where he's going to be for the rest of our lives relaxes me completely.

I doze off at some point, my head resting back against the seat, happier and more content than I've ever been in life. That's the last thought I have before disaster strikes.

CHAPTER FOURTEEN

Blake

This is a total fucking nightmare that I can't seem to wake up from. One minute we were cruising along the highway heading toward San Antonio, and the next we're hit hard from behind, so hard that I lose control of the truck and end up in a ditch by the side of the road.

I can tell immediately that I'm fine, but Honey... She won't wake up.

My phone flew out of the cup holder and is now on the floor of the passenger side. I can't seem to get my hands to work right as I wrestle my way out of the seat belt and try to reach my phone on the far side of the cab. My fingers close on it, and I focus on not dropping it. A knock on the window has me looking back over my shoulder.

The man outside pulls the driver side door open. "Y'all right, man? I saw the whole thing! Called 9-1-1."

"I'm fine, but my girl, she won't wake up." *This can't be happening again. Please God, not again. I won't survive it again. As much as I loved*

Jordan... No, just no. I can feel the hysteria forming in my chest, and suddenly I can't seem to get air to my lungs.

"Let's get you out of there," the guy outside says.

"No, not without her."

"I smell gas, man. You ought to get out. I'll help you with her."

"Shouldn't move her."

"Dude, you don't have a choice. This thing could blow at any second. Let's get you both out of there."

Other people materialize from outside, and, working together, we manage to remove Honey from the cab of my mangled truck. We get her settled far enough from the truck that no one will be harmed if it does go up in flames. She's so pale and lifeless, but the first guy assures me she's alive. "Feel right here," he says, grabbing my hand to press my fingers against the pulse point in her neck.

Feeling the strong beat of her heart makes me weep. I drop my head to her chest and beg her not to leave me. I want to feel her fingers sifting through my hair and hear her lusty laugh and watch her gorgeous eyes light up with love and pleasure and desire and a million other emotions. We just found each other. I can't lose her. I just can't.

The strangers who came to our rescue do what they can to console me in the endless time it takes for EMS to arrive in a frenzy of sirens and SUVs and ambulances. After the paramedics assess her condition, a decision is made to call in a chopper to transport her to a trauma center in San Antonio. That decision strikes absolute terror in my heart, even after the lead paramedic assures me that it's only because it'll be quicker than driving, not because she's in danger of dying.

You can't convince me. Even though it's over one hundred degrees outside, I'm cold all over. I can't stop shaking or recalling how beautifully, vibrantly alive she was just this morning when we got engaged.

"Blake." I turn to Clint, who was the first to help us.

"They want you to go with her." He points to the rescue helicopter that's landing about fifty feet from where I'm watching this surreal scene unfold like an all too familiar horror show. "I'll wait for the tow to get your truck. Don't worry about anything."

I want to laugh at the absurdity of that statement. *Don't worry about anything? Really?* But he's only trying to help, and he deserves my thanks, not my ridicule. "I... Thank you."

"Yeah, no problem. Go with her. I'll take care of the truck and make sure they find you to tell you where it is."

"Thanks." Following behind the gurney they've loaded Honey onto, I jog to the spot where the chopper team is waiting for the paramedics to load her up. The first responders give a shouted assessment to the chopper crew. I'm pulled into the helicopter by one of the crewmembers, and we lift off seconds later, before I can even catch my breath or process anything I just heard about possible closed head injuries or concussions or brain bleeds.

We land at University Hospital in San Antonio a few minutes after we take off, and Honey is whisked away by the doctors who meet us on the roof. No one tells me where they're taking her, so I run after them, hoping they'll let me stay with her.

A nurse stops me at the doors to the Emergency Department. She takes me into a cubicle to get some information about Honey. I tell them her name is Evelyn Carmichael, but she goes by Honey. I don't know what insurance she has. Shouldn't I know that? I'm her fucking *fiancé*. I can't remember her birthday, and that has me blinking back tears. What right do I have to her if I can't remember her fucking birthday?

I brush away the tears and try to focus on what Honey needs from me. "Let me call her friend. She'll know what I don't." I pull my phone from my pocket and dial Lauren's number from memory. It hasn't changed from when we used to hook up.

"Now why are you calling me when you're supposed to be on vacation with my best girl?" Lauren cheerfully asks when she answers.

"Lo."

"Blake? What? What's wrong?"

Somehow I manage to get the words out, to tell her where we are and what I need.

"I'm on my way. Put me on with the nurse. I'll tell her what I can."

"Thanks, Lo."

"Is she, tell me... Blake..."

"I don't know. I don't anything yet."

"I'm coming. I'll be there as fast as I can."

I nod because that's all I can do and hand the phone to the nurse, who asks Lauren a series of questions. I watch her write the March 2nd date on the chart, and commit that date to memory. I pray that she'll live to see another birthday.

———

LAUREN ARRIVES FIVE LONG HOURS LATER, WITH GARRETT IN TOW. I've never been so happy to see anyone as I am to see them when they find me in the ICU waiting room. I'm allowed in to see Honey once every half hour for a few minutes.

"What's the latest?" Lauren has called me for regular updates from the road, and I can't tell her anything more now than I could then.

"They say she's stable, and we have to wait and see."

"What does that *mean?*" Lauren's eyes are red from crying.

Garrett puts his arm around her to offer comfort she doesn't want. She shakes him off.

"That's all they've told me other than she has a severe concussion from the whiplash. We got hit hard from behind, and somehow she broke her ankle, too."

"And they checked you out?" Garrett asks.

"Yeah, I'm fine. They said it was because I was awake, if you can believe that. She was asleep, so she was defenseless." My voice catches as a sob erupts from my chest. "I can't believe this has happened again."

Lauren hugs me hard. "It's not like before. Honey is alive and fighting, and she's going to be fine. We have to believe that."

"Listen to her," Garrett says. "She's almost always right."

"There's no almost about it," Lauren insists. "I'm always right."

Their reassurances are the only thing keeping me from completely losing my mind.

———

It's after midnight when I talk Lauren and Garrett into leaving to find somewhere to spend the night. The ICU nurses take mercy on me and let me sit by Honey's bed.

I hold the hand that wears my ring, and I tell her about Lauren and Garrett showing up in San Antonio and how they went off to spend the night together, probably in the same room. I talk about all the things we're going to do after we're married. I tell her about the farm and the swimming hole and her photography and my construction and how we should put the two together to create a business we can run together, like the couple on HGTV that combined his renovation skills with her design flair. We could be like them, I tell her, and raise our little brood of blond-haired kids while working side by side.

I'm not sure what time it is when my parents appear outside the room, looking exhausted and upset and stressed. The glass walls make it hard to miss them standing out there, watching us.

I kiss the back of Honey's hand and place it gently on the bed. Then I walk over to the door and step outside to talk to my parents.

"We came as soon as we heard, son," Dad says as they both hug me. "Are you all right?"

"I will be as soon as Honey wakes up. I'm sorry I didn't call you myself." I asked Garrett to call them because I wasn't sure I could say the words without breaking into a million pieces.

"We understand," Mom says.

I run my fingers through my hair, certain it must be standing on end after hours of pulling on it. "I should tell you... While we were away, I asked Honey to marry me, and she said yes."

"Oh, Blake," Mom says, blinking back tears. "Oh, I've always loved Honey. That's such wonderful news! Isn't it wonderful, Mike?"

"It sure is." Dad's gaze shifts to the room, where Honey is attached to all kinds of machines. "Is she going to be okay?"

"They tell me she should be, but they aren't entirely sure yet. She's got a concussion and a broken ankle from her leg being jammed under the dash. The worst part..." I take a deep breath and force myself to stay calm. "She hasn't woken up yet."

Dad grasps my shoulder with his big hand. "Son, I can't imagine what must be running through your mind in light of what you've been through in the past. But this isn't like that. Jordan was killed instantly. She never stood a chance. Honey isn't Jordan." He takes me by the shoulders and turns me to face her. "Look at her. She's got a good strong heartbeat, and she just needs some rest before she'll wake up and ask you what all the fuss is about."

Tears roll down my cheeks. I want so badly to believe he's right, that this is nothing like the last time, but why won't she wake up? I wipe away the tears, determined to be strong for her the way she always is for me. But damn, I wish I could run away and hide, bury myself in work or something, anything to make this terrible ache go away.

But there's only one thing that can take away the ache, and that's Honey.

Mom and Dad sit with me for an hour before they go to sleep in the ICU waiting room. They refuse to leave me alone, probably because they're afraid of what I'll do if Honey doesn't make it—and with good reason. I can't bear to let my mind wander in that direction.

I return to my spot next to Honey's bed, holding her hand, stroking her hair and talking to her about everything and nothing, hoping the sound of my voice will bring her back to me.

Honey

I hear him. I smell his distinctive scent. I can feel his hand in mine and the touch of his fingers in my hair. I take comfort from the sound of his voice, even if I can't quite understand the things he's saying. I feel his love in every word and in every stroke of his skin against mine.

Where am I? What happened?

We're engaged. He asked me to marry him. I said yes. There was a ring, a nice ring with a big diamond.

I open my eyes, blinking when the bright light makes them water. I lick my lips, which are so dry they feel like they belong to someone else. My head hurts.

Blake's head is on the bed next to mine. I'd know that hair anywhere.

I want to touch him, but I can't seem to make anything work the way it's supposed to. My hand is trapped under his, and he's heavy on top of me. He's here. That's all that matters. For now.

I close my eyes, but only because I can't keep them open.

The next time I open them, Blake is standing next to the window, looking out at the bright sunshine. The slight slump of his shoulders tells me how exhausted he is, and I want to comfort him. My tongue feels too big for my mouth, which is so dry that it hurts. I want to drink in the sight of him, but my eyes won't stay open.

Frustrated, I make a sound and open my eyes again to see his blue eyes go wild as he looks down at me.

"Honey!" He takes my hand and brings it to his lips, his whiskers rough against my skin. "Darlin', wake up. Please wake up."

It takes everything I have to keep my eyes open, wincing at the bright light.

Blake goes to the window and closes the blinds. "Better?"

"Mmmhmm."

"Honey, sweetheart..."

I lick my lips. "Not what you call me."

He drops his head to rest on my hand. Is he crying?

"Blake..."

"I'm here, Honeydew. I'm right here."

"What happened?"

He looks up at me, his eyes ravaged from tears and exhaustion. "We were hit from behind on the highway. We went off the road. You have a concussion and a broken ankle. We've been waiting two days for you to wake up."

Two days? I try to process that, and then I gasp, thinking about how horrible that must've been for him after losing Jordan the way he did. I begin to cry. "So sorry to do that to you."

"Aww, Honeybee, don't cry." He wipes away my tears. "Please don't cry. The only thing that matters is that you're awake and talking to me and going to be all right."

I close my eyes because they won't stay open. "And I'm going to marry you."

"That, too," he says, kissing my hand and then leaning over me to kiss my lips.

"Thirsty."

Blake checks with the nurses, who give him permission to get me some ice chips, which are, officially, the best thing I've ever had in my entire life.

"So good. More."

"Take it easy. You don't want to make yourself sick by overdoing it."

"Were you hurt in the crash?"

"No."

"Have you been a mess?"

"Something like that. I couldn't believe it was happening again."

I wrap my hand around his, wincing when the IV fights back. "Totally different outcome this time."

"You couldn't tell me that the first day." He lets his head drop down to our joined hands as if it's too much for him to hold it up. "This guy named Clint came to our rescue out there. He helped me get you out of the truck, and then he came here to bring me our stuff."

"That's really nice of him."

"It was. He waited until they towed the truck and brought me info on where to find it. It's totaled, by the way."

"I'm so sorry. I know how much you love that truck."

"I don't give a fuck about the truck, Honey. It can be replaced. You..." He draws in a choppy breath. "You... You could never..." His voice breaks, and he shakes his head.

Though I'm moved by his emotional reaction, I go for a moment of levity. "You'd better not be replacing me."

"There's no replacing you, Honey Nut Cheerio."

CHAPTER FIFTEEN

Honey

I spend a week in the hospital in San Antonio before they clear me to go home. Lauren and Garrett are there for a couple of days, as are Blake's parents, but for most of the time, it's just the two of us, in my room, watching movies and eating the takeout he procures for us from all over the city. He says we need to take full advantage of our time here to try as many different places as we can.

The nurses have gotten used to finding him snuggled up to me in my bed, and they've stopped teasing us about celebrating our engagement in their hospital. They're all super nice to us, and I'm almost sad to say good-bye to them when Blake wheels me to the front door for the ride home.

His dad made the long trek back to San Antonio to drive us home. When I ask Blake why we didn't just rent a car, he says it was easier to have his dad come. I've left all the arrangements to him, so I don't question it further, but it does strike me as odd. I wonder if he's afraid to drive me myself, and I hope that isn't the case.

I sleep most of the five-hour ride home, mostly because I'm still on painkillers for my ankle that knock me out. The closer we get to home, the more anxious I become about having taken more than two weeks out of work. I've built up a cushion, but the downside of being self-employed is that if I'm not working, there's no money coming in.

I need to get back to it as soon as I can, but with a bulky cast on my ankle and crutches for the next six weeks, I'm not sure how I'll manage. If I think too much about the realities of my situation, my anxiety spikes into the red zone. Along with the house that I own free and clear, Gran left me with a nice little nest egg that I've never touched. I pretend like I don't have that money, but I may need to tap into it if I can't get back to scheduling photo shoots again soon.

"What's the matter?" Blake asks from his seat in the front.

"What do you mean?"

"When you're worrying about something, you do this thing with your lips. You've been doing it for half an hour now."

"I do? I have?" Has anyone ever paid closer attention to me than he does? No one, except for Gran, of course. I realize how much I've missed being "seen" the way he sees me.

He nods. "What's on your mind?"

I glance at his dad, who's focused on the road and not on us. Then I look back at Blake. "Let's talk when we get home."

His curt nod tells me he's not happy to put it off, but he understands my desire for privacy.

We arrive at my house late in the afternoon. Even though I slept for most of the ride, I'm tired and sore, and I still have a headache that won't quit. Blake seems to know what I need. He scoops me up from the backseat and carries me into the house.

"Thank you for coming to get us, Mike."

"Any time, Honey. Happy to see you home safe."

I'm surprised to see a shiny new black truck bearing Blake's company logo in my driveway. "Where'd that come from?"

"Garrett took care of picking up a new one for me."

"You never said if they got the guy who hit us."

"They got him. He was drunk."

I shudder at the thought of how much worse it could've been for both of us. "I'm so sorry you had to go through this."

"Don't apologize to me. None of it is your fault."

I try not to focus on his sharp tone or gruff demeanor. I chalk it up to post-accident stress and his worries about getting me home and settled. Things will calm down and return to normal now that I'm home. I'm sure of it.

He sets me gently on the bed, props my ankle on a pillow and covers me with a blanket. "Comfortable?"

I extend a hand to him. "I'd be more comfy if you joined me."

He takes my hand, gives it a squeeze and releases it. "I need to run home to pick up a few things and hit the store to get us stocked up. Lauren is going to come by to stay with you while I'm gone."

"I don't need a babysitter. I'm fine by myself."

"You're recovering from a head injury and managing on crutches. You *do* need a babysitter, so don't argue with me."

There's that gruff tone again. I chalk it up to the stress he's been under, but I begin to worry that it might be something more than that.

"Fine. Whatever you want."

"What were you stressing out about in the car?"

"My business and the lack of revenue when I'm not working."

"Don't worry about that. I'll take care of anything you need."

"That's not what I want, and it's not why I told you."

"Please, Honey. Don't worry about it. I'm going to go, but I'll be back."

I don't have the energy to argue about anything, including money. "Okay."

He turns and leaves the room. I try not to notice that he doesn't kiss me or tell me he loves me the way he would have only last week before the crash.

I must've dozed off, because the next thing I know, Lauren is in my room, fussing over the blankets and arranging a vase with my favorite black-eyed Susans. "Thank you." My voice sounds rough with sleep and the thirst I can't seem to quench no matter how much water I drink. The nurses told me it's because of all the medication I've been on.

Lauren is right there with a cup of ice water. She holds the straw for me.

"Thanks."

"It's nice to have you home."

"It's nice to be home." I push myself up, looking for a more comfortable position, the pain in my head taking my breath away for a second.

"You're still in a lot of pain. I hate to see that."

"It's better than it was."

"Can I get you anything?"

"A new head would be awesome."

Despite her smile, I see the exhaustion and worry etched into her pretty face. I reach for her hand.

She folds her hand into mine.

"I'm okay, Lo. I promise."

"Scared me," she whispers. "Getting that phone call was like Jordan all over again."

"I know. It must've been awful for all of you."

"It was. Thank God for Garrett. He showed up right after I got the call and offered to drive me to San Antonio. He was amazing through the whole thing."

"Is that so?" I ask with a suggestive smile.

"Yeah, he was great."

"Blake said you guys got a hotel together."

"We did. We even slept in the same bed. Platonically."

"Well, that's a shame. I would've thought you'd use my unfortunate accident to further your agenda where he's concerned."

"Very funny. I was too undone over you to even think about jumping his bones."

"Is this the same girl who coached me to walk into a bar and ask Blake to fuck me? You disappoint me."

"Ha-ha, very funny. I was traumatized after seeing my best friend in a coma. Give a girl a break, will you?"

I roll my eyes at her, even though it hurts to do that. "I was never in a coma."

"Well, you were out of it for days. Very *long* days. I thought Blake would lose his mind waiting for you to wake up."

"He seems... off... Have you noticed that?"

"Garrett and I both noticed he's extremely stressed out. He'll be better now that you're home."

"I hope so." I debate whether I should say more, because saying it out loud makes it official. "It's just that before the accident, he was so happy. We got engaged and were making plans and everything was great. And now..."

"What?" she asks, her brows furrowing.

"He's saying and doing all the right things, but he reminds me of the guy I picked up in a bar who wanted to keep his distance at all costs. He's nothing at all like the guy he'd been lately."

"He's crazy about you, Honey. The whole town is talking about you guys getting married. You've got to give him some time to get past the accident and the trauma of seeing you hurt so badly. Think about what he's been through in the past and how that must've affected him."

"That's all I can think about. Jordan's death turned him into an emotionless shell of a man. I can't bear to see him go back to that again, Lo." My eyes fill with tears. "I can't lose him to the past, not after everything we've shared."

"Give it some time. Let him recover with you. In a couple of weeks, things will be back to normal. You'll see."

I glom on to Lauren's reassurances, but deep down inside, I'm afraid I lost *him* in that crash.

———

BY THE END OF MY SECOND WEEK AT HOME, I'M GOING STIR-CRAZY. I want to get back to work in the worst way, but I have two more days before my appointment with my regular doctor, who will, hopefully, give me the all clear to return to work on a limited basis. My ankle has gone from hurting to itching, and I'm able now to put some weight on it and hobble around without the crutches.

With my plan to resume half days next week, I contact some of the customers who were forced to wait for me to recover to reschedule their appointments. I can't wait to get back to cranky babies and bossy mothers. That's my normal, and I'm craving it.

Blake has been so busy dealing with the work backlog he came home to that I barely see him except for when he crawls into bed next to me, many nights after midnight. I can't help but feel that he's avoiding me, our relationship, our engagement, our future. Our physical relationship has become a chaste peck on the cheek before he leaves for work each morning. That's it. He hardly ever touches me otherwise, which is not at all like the passionate man I fell in love with.

I'm trying to take Lauren's advice and give him some time, but I'm beginning to fear that there's no bridging the gulf the crash has put between us.

Garrett stops by late one afternoon, knocking on the door before coming in with yet another bouquet of flowers. Over the last few weeks, I've suspected he brings me flowers as an excuse to stop by Lauren's shop, but he's never said so, and I haven't asked. Not that I'm above giving them a nudge, but it has to be done correctly. In my opinion, they'd make a great couple, and if I get the chance, I'm going to give him a subtle push in her direction.

Garrett has dark hair and eyes and a gorgeous smile. We went out a couple of times in high school, and nothing other than friendship ever came of it, but I've always thought he was super cute and sweet. He sits on one of Gran's fussy little parlor chairs that's way too small for his strapping frame. "I feel like I'm going to break this thing by sitting on it."

"You very well might. Blake calls it dollhouse furniture."

"I can see why. How're you feeling, Honey?"

"Stir-crazy, ready to get back to work and my life. Otherwise, not bad."

"Speaking of work, that's why I stopped by."

"If it's awful, don't tell me."

He smiles, which only makes him cuter than he already is. "It's not awful. I took the liberty of liquidating one of your CDs that came up for maturity this month, which gives you two months' operating capital to pay this month's bills and next, too."

"Oh, Garrett, thank you so much for taking care of that. I've been freaking out about money, among other things."

"You're all set. Don't worry. I'm keeping an eye on things."

"Thank God for you. You can't ever move away."

"I'm not going anywhere."

I've known Garrett as long as I've known Blake, Lauren, Matt and Julie, so I'm hoping he'll take what I'm about to say the right way. "I want to thank you for bringing Lauren to me when I needed her in San Antonio."

"I was happy to be able to help in some way. She was a disaster. I couldn't let her drive five hours in that condition."

"It was good of you to look out for her."

"That's what friends do."

"So you guys are friends? *Just* friends?"

"What're you up to, Honey?" he asks with a grin.

"Nothing. Much..."

"We're good friends. Always have been, always will be."

"But that's it?" I ask, my heart sinking.

"I never said that."

"Don't be coy with me, Garrett McKinley. She's my best friend, and she has a crush on you." So much for subtlety. I smack a hand over my mouth. "*OhmyGod.*" The hand I keep over my big mouth muffles my voice. "I can't believe I said that out loud. It's the concussion. Has to be."

He looks like he's been poleaxed. "She has a crush. On *me*?"

With the hand still in place over my mouth, I nod.

"Is this a recent development?"

I shake my head.

"Well, I'll be damned."

I finally unseal my mouth. "Is this good news?"

"It's not bad news. I like her a lot. I always have."

"But?"

"No buts. I like her."

"She thinks you think she's an airhead." In for a penny...

"What? I do not!"

"I told her that was ridiculous. Look at the business she runs and all the stuff she does for the needy and the elderly."

"I don't think that about her at all. I think she's amazing."

"Maybe somehow you could find a way to tell *her* that?"

"Yeah," he says, seeming rattled. "I will." He leans forward, elbows on knees. "You know the main reason why I've never asked her out?"

"I have no clue."

"She used to be with Blake, and he's one of my best friends. I thought it might be weird between him and me if I pursued her, even if it was a long time ago for them."

"That's the same reason I never thought about dating him, but she told me to quit being ridiculous. That was ages ago, after she finally left Wayne. She deserved to be with a decent guy like Blake after what she went through with Wayne."

He cringes at the mention of Lauren's ex-husband. "I hope that guy never shows his face around here again."

"He'd be crazy to step foot in Marfa. He has to know half the town wants to see him dead for daring to lay hands on her."

"I'd be first in line," he says fiercely, so fiercely that I realize he hasn't been immune to her at all, but rather the exact opposite. "She really has a crush on me?" he asks hopefully.

"She really does, but you did *not* hear that from me."

"Hear what?" he asks with a wink.

"As long as we're telling secrets, what's going on with your buddy Blake?"

He seems genuinely baffled. "What do you mean?"

"You haven't noticed a change in him since the accident?"

"Other than being frantically busy at work and worrying about you, no, not really."

"Well, I have."

"How so?"

"He's different, remote like he used to be, not at all affectionate, and he's making up excuses to be anywhere but here except to sleep. I keep asking him to take me out for a ride or dinner or anything to get out of here, but he always has a reason why he can't."

"Huh, that's odd."

Hearing him confirm it doesn't do much to comfort me. I rub my hand over the ache in my chest that's becoming more intense by the day. "Something's wrong, Garrett. Lauren told me to give him time and space to get back to normal after the accident, but it's been weeks, and he's more withdrawn by the day. Will you talk to him and see if you can figure out what's going on with him?"

"Of course."

I breathe a sigh of relief. "And you won't tell him I sent you?"

"He won't hear that from me."

"Thank you, Garrett."

He grins at me. "Least I can do for you after you opened my eyes to a few things I needed to know."

CHAPTER SIXTEEN

Blake

I line up the Weedwacker at the base of the granite stone and turn it on, knocking down the tall grass that's grown around Jordan's gravestone while I've been too busy to tend to it the way I normally do.

Normal.

What does that even mean anymore? For a long time, my normal was work, work and more work, with an occasional meaningless screw thrown in there to keep me sane. Then Honey came into the bar and propositioned me, turning my orderly world upside down. It was fun for a while, until reality intruded to remind me that nothing lasts forever, and it's easier not to get involved than to risk losing everything.

The buzz of the Weedwacker is oddly comforting as I clean up Jordan's gravesite and the one belonging to her grandparents next to her. I'm ashamed of how overgrown they've gotten while I was too busy to tend to them. I hope her grandparents would approve of the work I'm doing to their house. I'm back to thinking I'll sell it when it's finished. Living there with Honey and the family we might've had together was nothing more than a pipe dream. I know that now.

Once she's fully recovered, I'll tell her in the gentlest way possible that I've changed my mind about us. I'd rather be alone for the rest of my life than ever go through what I did on that highway outside of San Antonio. Not to mention the endless days in the hospital when I didn't know if she would ever wake up and look at me with those gorgeous brown eyes or smile at me in that special way she saves just for me.

I shake off those thoughts. They're counterproductive. There's no sense yearning for things that can never be. I'm far better off focusing on the work that has sustained me for all these years.

She'll be disappointed, but she'll get over it. An amazing woman like Honey won't be single for long. Some great guy will snap her up and give her all the things I can't. I was an absolute fool to think I'd moved far enough past what happened to Jordan to take another chance with Honey.

And if the thought of her with another guy makes me want to commit murder? Well, that'll pass in time. Her happiness is the most important thing, and I don't have what it takes to make myself happy, let alone anyone else.

For a couple of beautiful months, I deluded myself into believing I'd recovered from the trauma of losing Jordan. Drunk on the hottest sex of my life, I thought I was better now, ready to try again, but that turned out to be utter bullshit. While standing on that highway, fearing that I'd already lost her forever, I found out how not ready I am for anything remotely like the things I wanted with Honey.

I can't afford to care that much about anyone, and Honey deserves better than a shell of a man who hasn't got a goddamned thing to give her.

I'm startled out of my increasingly dire thoughts by the sight of Garrett, walking across the grass that leads to Jordan's plot in the local cemetery. What the hell is he doing here? And how did he find me? Annoyed to be interrupted, I turn off the machine and raise the goggles that cover my eyes. "What're you doing here?"

"Looking for you."

"Well, you found me."

"Surprised to find you here. I figured you'd be home with Honey by now."

"Got stuff to do. This place doesn't keep itself up on its own."

"No, it doesn't, but no one says you have to be the only one to do it."

"I've always done it, and I always will, as long as I'm on this side of the grass."

"Okay."

"That all you came to say?"

"Actually, no. I guess I'm sort of wondering why you're back to burying yourself in work when you have a fiancée waiting for you at home."

"In case you didn't notice, I was away for two weeks. I had a few things to do when I came home."

"You were caught up after the first week you were back, so I'm afraid you're going to have to do better than that."

"What do you want me to say?"

"I want you to tell me what's wrong."

"Everything is wrong! I fucked up with Honey. I never should've proposed to her, and now I have to undo it, and that fucking kills me."

"Then don't undo it."

"I have to."

"Why? Why do you have to?"

"Because." I can hear the utter misery in my own voice, and I have no doubt my close friend can hear it, too.

"I have a theory I'd like to run by you. You can tell me if I'm hot, cold or even lukewarm."

I don't want to hear his theory, but I doubt that'll stop him from sharing it.

"Twelve years ago, something awful happened to all of us, but mostly to you and Jordan's family, the people who loved her best."

Because I don't trust myself to hold it together, I take an intense interest in the grass.

"That was a terrible time, and for years, you coped with your loss and the guilt associated with it by throwing yourself into your work.

The only pleasure you allowed yourself was a beer at the end of the day, an occasional roll in the hay and limited time with your family and friends. Am I warm?"

I shrug. He's hot as hell, but I'm not going to tell him that.

"Then you got together with Honey, and for a while, everything seemed better. You were laughing again like you hadn't laughed in a dozen years, smiling, joking, taking chances, making plans."

"And look at where that landed me, back in another motherfucking hospital."

"Ahhh, and here we get to the heart of the matter, the horrible, terrible thing that almost happened again. The key word being *almost*. Honey's not dead, Blake. She's alive and well and in love with you and wondering why you're spending your time everywhere but with her."

"She tell you that?"

"She didn't have to tell me. I went to her house to see you both. You weren't there, and she didn't know when you'd be home. You weren't at the bar or your house, so I came out here. Now you tell me why anyone would rather spend time at the cemetery than home with the woman he loves, the woman who loves him."

"You don't get it!" I want to wrap my hands around his neck and strangle the life out of him. How dare he try to expose me this way? I thought he was my friend.

"Don't tell me I don't get it. I've lived every second of this journey along with you. I've watched you go from a happy, carefree, optimistic young man to an empty shell of a man who thinks the only way to get through each day is to power through. That is no way to live, Blake, and the Jordan I knew and loved wouldn't want that for you."

"Don't you dare pretend to know what she would want."

"Why not? You weren't the only one who loved her. We all did. I knew her my whole life, and that sweet, loving girl would not want you to use her death as an excuse to run away from life."

"That's not what I'm doing."

"Isn't it? Isn't it what you've been doing so long now that you don't know how to do anything else when another accident rocks your world and makes you think—stupidly—that the only way to live is to take zero chances?"

I'm afraid if I say anything, I might end a lifelong friendship, so I maintain my stony silence.

Garrett takes a step closer, his voice softer when he says, "Look, I feel for you, man. Everyone does. How could something like that happen to one guy twice in a lifetime, but you know what else has happened to you twice in a lifetime?"

Forcing my gaze up to meet his, I raise a brow.

"True love. Hasn't happened yet for me, so I'm envious that you've had it twice. If I were you and I had an amazing woman like Honey crazy in love with me, I'd hold on to her with everything I had."

I want to. God knows I want to, but I can't. "Well, you're not me."

"No, I'm not, and I can't possibly fathom what it was like for you not knowing if Honey was going to make it. But she did, and how sad would it be if she went through everything she did to survive only to lose you because some idiot got drunk and decided it would be a good idea to hit the road? How is that fair to her?"

It isn't fair, and I didn't need Garrett to point that out to me.

"I feel for her, you know?" Garrett said. "I mean, she was already abandoned by the most important person in her life the day she was born. I'd hate to see that happen to her again."

"I'm not abandoning her." But as I say the words, I feel like a knife is twisting in my chest as I recall her expressing her fear of that very thing. Isn't that exactly what I'm planning to do? "She'll be fine."

"Maybe she will. Maybe she won't. Hard to know for sure. I'll say one more thing, and then I'll let you get back to work." He waits until I'm looking at him before he says, "I sure did like having my old friend Blake around the last couple of months. I hadn't realized how much I'd missed him."

Leaving me reeling, Garrett walks away, hands in his pockets and head down on the way to his truck. I want to run after him, to tell him he's got it all wrong, that he doesn't really understand, but I remain rooted to the spot where he found me, next to my dead girlfriend's grave while the fiancée I plan to break up with waits for me at home.

When did my life get so fucked up?

Honey

At the end of my first week back to work, Lauren brings dinner over, and we eat it on the sofa while watching *Steel Magnolias* on TV. We lose our shit during the scene where Sally Field's character freaks out at the cemetery after burying her daughter. We sob our heads off like a couple of fools. But then I'm not crying because Sally's daughter died. I'm crying because at some point in the last couple of weeks, I lost Blake, and I have no idea how I'm going to survive without him.

My heart is broken into a million pieces, and he's the only one who can put me back together. But he doesn't want me anymore. He's even stopped bothering to slip into bed with me at night. I haven't seen him in three days.

Lauren realizes this meltdown has nothing to do with the movie and wraps her arms around me, holding me while I cry it out.

"I don't understand what happened," I say between sobs. The ring that still sits on my finger is a painful reminder of the best days of my life. "We were so happy when we left South Padre. It was perfect, until the accident happened and ruined everything."

"I'm so sorry, Honey. I wish I knew what to say to make you feel better."

"I can't believe it's over. I keep hoping he's going to show up and miraculously be the man he was the last couple of months, but that's not going to happen, is it?"

"I wish I knew. Garrett talked to him, and he thinks the accident triggered memories, and Blake is doing what he did before to survive by retreating into his work to avoid having to deal with the pain of nearly losing you."

"He didn't lose me! I'm right here, wishing he were here with me. No offense to you, of course."

"None taken," she says with a kind smile as she brushes the hair back from my face. "I have an idea. I'm not sure if it's the right thing to do, but it worked once before, so who's to say it won't work again?"

Desperate to hear any ideas she might have, I wipe away my tears and take a big drink from my wineglass.

"What if you were to go find him and use the line that started this whole thing one more time?"

I shake my head. "He doesn't want anything to do with me. What makes you think he'll want to do that?"

"He wants everything with you, Honey. He just can't give himself permission to take what he wants because he feels responsible for you getting hurt, for Jordan being killed. You have to overpower him with reminders of what he'd be giving up if he lets you go." She takes my hand and looks directly into my eyes. "You need to be strong enough for both of you."

"I don't know if I am, though. I don't feel strong at all."

"You, Honey Carmichael, are the strongest person I've ever met. Look at the things you've already overcome in your life, things that would've broken a lesser person. If you want this man as much as I think you do, then you have to fight for him by reminding him of what's at stake."

Lauren's faith in me brings new tears to my eyes. "What if he turns me down?"

"Then you'll have the answer you need and can move forward knowing you did everything you could. Think about it."

I wonder how I'll think about anything else.

———

Two days later, I've run out of excuses for why I can't do what Lauren suggested. I miss Blake so much that I'm willing to potentially humiliate myself if it means I get to see that handsome face and those amazing blue eyes one more time.

After work, I remove the walking boot I'm supposed to wear at least twelve hours a day for the next month, take a shower and spend extra time on my hair and makeup. I stand in front of my closet for easily half an hour before I choose a white minidress that's quite possibly the sexiest thing I own because it leaves absolutely nothing to the imagination—not that Blake has to imagine me naked. He's seen the real thing often enough.

I top off the outfit with my favorite red cowboy boots and quickly decide my healing ankle isn't ready for boots. I replace them with low-heeled sandals nowhere near as fun as the boots, but at least they don't hurt to wear. Finally, I spray perfume in all the most important places.

Then I kill a couple of hours by watching mindless TV until I'm sure it's late enough that he'll be home.

The drive to his house feels endless even if it takes only fifteen minutes. As I pull into his driveway, I'm flooded with memories of the night I followed him home and everything that came after. I want him back, and I'm determined to do everything I can to convince him that we can make this work if only he'd give us a fighting chance.

His house is dark, and since he parks in the garage, I have no way to know for sure if he's actually home, but I've come too far to turn back now.

My palms are sweaty as I walk up to the front door and ring the doorbell, listening to it chime throughout the house. I wait for what feels like an eternity before I ring the bell again, waiting and listening for footsteps that don't come.

Either he's not home or he's not answering the door. I choose the former and decide I'm not going so far as to use the code he gave me the night I brought him home drunk. Where else would he be at this hour? I have to think about that for only a second before I know exactly where I'll find him.

Mindful of my fragile ankle, I walk slowly back to the car when I'd much rather run. I drive carefully, adhere to the speed limit and keep my eyes and attention on the road, as another accident is the very last thing I need right now. I take the last turn before the farm, and in the distance, I see the lights burning on the first floor.

My heart gives a happy leap. I'm going to see him in a few minutes, and I can't wait. I give myself a little pep talk on the way down the driveway to the house. "No matter what happens, you'll be fine. With him or without him, you'll be okay." But oh, I so hope I'll be with him.

I pull up next to his truck, turn off the car and extinguish the head-lights. No doubt he saw me coming, so there's no point in dragging this out. Gathering all the courage I possess, I run my fingers through my hair, apply a fresh coat of lipstick and head for the front porch.

He meets me at the door, his eyes widening at the sight of me. "Honey. What're you doing here?"

"Looking for you. May I come in?" Gran would be proud. She scrubbed the far more common "can I" from my vocabulary when I was a little girl.

"Um, yeah, sure. I guess."

I pretend not to notice his decided lack of enthusiasm as I brush past him into the house, which is much further along than it had been the last time I was here. The kitchen cabinets are in, gorgeous copper countertops have been laid, and there's even a sofa in the living room. I wonder if he's been sleeping here rather than with me.

"It looks fantastic, Blake. I love the countertops."

"Do you? I wasn't sure about them, but the lady at the showroom talked me into them."

"They're perfect. And the backsplash is so cool. Did you have to place every one of those little tiles by hand?"

"They come on twelve-by-twelve sheets."

"Oh, that's good. You'd be cross-eyed if you tried to do them one at a time. Show me what else you've done."

He reluctantly, or so it seems to me, leads me upstairs to the master suite, where the walls have been sheet-rocked and the original wood floors restored to gleaming glory. "This door is from the original barn," he says as he slides it to the left to reveal the master bathroom.

"Oh my God, look at that tub! It's amazing."

"I know how much you love your tub, so I got the biggest one they had. I figured whoever lives here would appreciate it."

Whoever lives here... I try not to let that statement derail my determination.

I run a hand over the white marble countertop on the double vanity. And then I turn to him, forcing him to meet my gaze. He looks so exhausted that I want to wrap my arms around him and offer him a place to rest, but I'm not sure I still have the right to do that. "I thought *we* were going to live here. Wasn't that the plan?"

He looks down at the floor, the agony in his expression shredding what's left of my heart. "Honey..."

"I want you to fuck me."

His head whips up, his eyes go wide, and his beautiful lips part in stunned amazement.

It takes everything I have, every ounce of faith in the love I feel for this man and the love I know he still feels for me, to close the distance between us, to place my hands on his chest and to look up at him looking down at me with blatant desire.

"I need you, Blake. I miss you so much, I ache from missing you. I miss your hands on me, your lips on me, your cock, your gorgeous abs, the way you look at me when you make love to me. I miss *everything* about us."

I had more to say, but it's hard to talk with someone else's tongue in your mouth. Yep, you heard me right, he's kissing my face off. He's completely unhinged, as if someone threw gas on a fire, and it feels like coming home. I wrap my arms around his neck and lose myself to the thrill of being back in his arms.

"Honey, wait, we should talk..."

"No, we shouldn't." I free the button to his jeans and unzip him quickly, before he can tell me all the reasons why this is a bad idea. To me, it feels like the best idea I've ever had, right up there with the first time we did this. I tuck my hand into his jeans and wrap it around his hard cock.

He hisses, and his head falls back. "Honey..."

"Make love to me, Blake. Please. I need you so bad."

"Your head... You're injured."

"I'm totally fine. I'm right here in your arms, and I want you." I keep a tight grip on him as I stroke him.

I hear his resistance crumble when all the air seems to leave his body in one long whoosh. And then he's lifting me and leaning me against the wall. I have no choice but to let go of his cock, which is now pressing against the place where I want him most.

"You forgot to wear panties under this handkerchief you've got on," he says on a low growl.

"Did I?" I give him a coy smile as I grasp a handful of his hair and give it a tug. "Don't go easy on me."

He slams home, and I scream from the pleasure, the pain, the burn and the absolute *rightness* of having him back where he belongs. I hope he knows I'll never let him go again.

"Honey... God, *Honey*."

The words, whispered roughly against my ear, travel through me like an electrical current. "I love you so much, Blake, and I always will. There's nothing that could make me stop loving you."

After that, there are no more words as we move together in perfect harmony. He reaches down to where we're joined and strokes me to an explosive finish. He's right there with me, surging into me over and over again until he sags against me, breathing hard as he holds me tight against him.

I take his face in my hands and kiss him everywhere I can reach, hoping I'm loving him enough for both of us. I'm afraid of what'll happen next, so I tighten my legs around his waist, keeping him anchored to me so he can't get away. My ankle throbs in protest of the position, but I ignore it.

Speaking softly, I open my heart to him. "I want to live here with you. I want to help you bring this place back to life. I want to bring *you* back to life. I want this ring you put on my finger and the life you asked me to share with you. I want to live that life fearlessly, not stuck in a past we cannot change, no matter how much we might wish we could. I want blond-haired babies with you, chickens in the yard and horses in the barn. I want a garden where we grow strawberries and green beans and cucumbers and tomatoes. I want summer days at the swimming hole and winter nights in our bed in this room that we'll make our own. I want holidays and birthdays. I want cookouts and family dinners. I want good times, bad times, joy and sorrow and every single thing with you. Only you."

He's quiet for such a long time that I begin to fear I haven't done enough to convince him.

Then he raises his head off my shoulder and looks into my eyes. "I'm powerless to resist you, Honeybee. God knows I tried."

"Stop trying." Keeping my hands on his face, I look into his eyes.

"I'm sorry if the accident reminded you too much of things you'd rather forget. But it wasn't your fault that I got hurt. Tell me you know that."

"I'm not quite there yet."

"Luckily, we have the rest of our lives to get you there."

"I have this dark place inside me, Honey. I can't always predict when it'll drag me down."

"You don't have to predict it. I'll be here to raise you up when the darkness tries to take you down."

He strokes my cheek with his finger. "I'm sorry I walked away from us."

"You didn't go far."

"Will you always come after me if I forget to come home?"

"Count on it."

He nuzzles my neck. "And when we fight, will you ask me to fuck you so we can get things back on track?"

"Of course I will. It works every time."

His laughter is the sweetest sound I've ever heard, and then he tops that with his words. "I love you, Honeydew melon. And I always will."

EPILOGUE

One year later...

Honey

I'm using one of my new backdrops for this very special shoot. It's a photo I took one night when Blake and I drove out to Mitchell Flat to view the Marfa Magical Lights, or the ghost lights. People call them different things, but they're always magical to me. The image is blown up to cover most of one wall in the studio.

Over the years, I've taken hundreds, perhaps a thousand, photos of the lights, but on that particular night, I got the best shots ever. They form the backdrop for my first shoot with Matt and Julie's baby girl, Grace, who's now three months old and dressed in a cactus costume I made just for her, so her photos will be one of a kind, like her.

Julie beams with happiness as she helps Scarlett and me settle the baby against the props that will artfully hold her in place for the pictures. By the time we're finished here, Grace will seem to be one with the lights and the desert that surrounds our West Texas town.

Grace is in a great mood, smiling for the camera like she was born to model. "She's a natural," I tell her mom.

"I bet you say that about all of them," Julie says.

I adjust one of the lights to my liking. "Trust me, I don't."

"Trust me, she doesn't," Blake says when he joins us, slipping an arm around me from behind as he kisses my cheek. "I worried that we'd never have one of our own because she works with so many cranky babies." He flattens his hand possessively over my basketball-size baby bump, sending a thrill coursing through me. His possessiveness is still an instant turn-on.

"Hi there," I say to my smiling, handsome husband, who now comes to me every night after work rather than the bar he used to frequent. We've been married ten months and living in our dream house at the farm for six of those months. Because I couldn't bear to part with it, we rent out Gran's house to tourists who come to town for the various festivals and art shows. I never imagined this kind of happiness existed, and I certainly didn't expect to ever find it for myself. Propositioning him was the best thing I've ever done in my life —both times.

"You're not spending too much time on your feet, are you?"

"Nope. Grace is making it easy on me."

Lauren comes bursting through the front door as Garrett comes in the back. We still aren't sure if they're together or not, but they often seem to be in the same place at the same time, even if they don't use the same door.

"Did we miss it?" Lauren asks, brightening when she sees Grace in her cactus costume. "Oh my God! She's the cutest baby *ever*."

We all think so, probably because she's the first baby born to our group of friends, and we're smitten. I can't wait to add to the family when ours arrives in another week or two.

"Look at that smile," Garrett says, dazzled by the little girl. To Matt, he says, "I hope you've got a stick to keep the boys away."

Matt scowls. "She's not allowed to date until she's forty."

The rest of us snort with laughter. Our laughter delights Grace, and I capture every gummy grin on film. If only every shoot could go as smoothly as this one has. "I think we're done."

"That fast?" Julie asks.

"Yep. Your daughter is a star, and we nailed it."

Julie goes to collect the baby while the rest of us gather around the oversized monitor on my desk to look at the pictures.

Her parents are blown away. "I don't know how you do it, Honey," Julie says, sounding teary, "but she actually looks as if she's sitting in the desert with the lights behind her."

"That's the idea."

"It's amazing," Matt says.

"I'm so glad you're happy."

Julie hugs me. "I can't thank you enough for these priceless memories. We'll treasure the pictures always."

"Aww, stop. You're going to make me cry."

"Doesn't take much," Blake mutters, making the others laugh.

I smile at him, and the fierce love I see in his eyes takes my breath away. Fighting for him was the best thing I've ever done, and I've been reaping the benefits every day since.

"I'm buying dinner for everyone," Matt announces.

After some debate, it's decided we're going to Planet Marfa.

"We'll be right behind you," Blake says. "I'm going to help Honey get the studio ready for tomorrow morning."

"We'll save your seats," Scarlett says.

When we're alone, Blake puts his arms around me and draws me in close. "There. That's what I needed."

"Better than an after-work beer?"

"Better than anything has ever been."

I take his hand and place it under mine on my belly. "And about to get even better."

"Thank you for this incredible life you've given me, Honeymoon."

I hold on tight to him, my heart, my soul, my rock, my love, my everything. "Just think, all it took were six little words."

"Six little words that changed everything."

———

Keep reading for a sneak peek of Garrett and Laura's story in *Sex God*!

Thank you for reading *Sex Machine*! I hope you enjoyed Blake and Honey's story as much as I enjoyed writing it. I started this story more than five years ago and wrote a big chunk of it in one weekend. But then other stories demanded my time, and I never went back to it. Lately, I found myself wondering whatever became of Blake and Honey after she said those six little words to him. Now we know! Join the Sex Machine Reader Group at *https://www.facebook.com/groups/Machine-ReaderGroup/* to chat about the book.

I expect that readers will want to know if this was truly a standalone story or if I plan to return to Marfa for more stories. The most important element of writing books is that the story has to call to me in order for me to devote weeks and months to writing and publishing it. If Marfa calls to me in the future, I'll happily return to write more. We'll see what happens!

In the meantime, there's more to come in all of my ongoing series, and they're keeping me pretty busy.

Thanks to my behind-the-scenes team who help me with so many things every day: Julie Cupp, CMP, Lisa Cafferty, CPA, Holly Sullivan, Isabel Sullivan, Cheryl Serra and Nikki Colquhoun. To my beta readers, Anne Woodall and Kara Conrad, thank you for being my first readers. Thank you to my editorial team of Linda Ingmanson and Joyce Lamb, and to Kristina Brinton for the stunning cover of *Sex Machine*. I love those abs! My thanks go to the team at Sullivan & Partners for handling marketing and publicity for me.

As always, thank you to the readers who make this job so much fun. I appreciate each and every one of you!

xoxo

Marie

SEX GOD

Chapter One

Garrett

"I married the first man who made me come," Lauren says matter-of-factly, "and we all know how *that* turned out."

The chicken wing I'm about to stuff in my face is now suspended in midair as her words sink into my sex-starved brain. "*Wayne Peterson* was the first guy to make you come?"

"Don't judge me." She licks the barbecue sauce from her wing before she takes a dainty bite. I'm fascinated by the way she eats a wing without getting even a smudge of sauce on her lips, whereas I feel like I've taken a bath in the stuff. "I didn't even know what an orgasm was until Wayne gave me one."

Fascinated, I lean in closer. "How'd he do it?"

"Tongue," she says, also leaning in so she can't be overheard. In Marfa, Texas, someone is always listening. "I also didn't know people did...*that*...until Wayne did it to me."

This makes me laugh because she's so damned cute as she says it. "I was fourteen when I caught Tommy going down on Debbie in the basement family room. I had no idea what they were doing until I saw his tongue out and his face all slimy. She was squealing like a pig and pulling his hair. I thought it was the grossest thing I'd ever seen."

She sputters with laughter. "Oh my God! Did he know you saw them?"

"Nope." My brother, three years older than me, surely would've killed me, if for no other reason than I'd gotten an eyeful of his precious Debbie's bush and tits. They've been married close to ten years now and live in California, which means all the responsibility for my dad's business, our mother and younger siblings falls to me while my older brother lives large on the West Coast. That's a sore subject I try not to think too much about.

"Well, you were way ahead of me in figuring that one out."

Since she never, ever talks about the ex-husband who knocked her around on his way out of town to parts unknown, I take this opportunity to dig a little deeper. "So before it went bad with him, it was good?"

"Nah, it was never good. I think he made me come three times in total. He was always an asshole, but he didn't become a violent asshole until six months after I made the huge mistake of marrying him."

The thought of gigantic Wayne Peterson getting rough with tiny Lauren makes me fucking furious. "I hope you know there're a lot of guys in this town who'd love five minutes alone in a room with that son of a bitch."

She takes a drink from her bottle of Bud, her eyes shining warmly at me. "You're very sweet to say so."

"I mean it. If I ever lay eyes on that asshole again, I'll show him what it feels like to get the shit kicked out of him." And I could do it, too. I might push paper for a living, but I work out like a fiend. That's one of several ways I deal with the stress of being stuck in a life I never signed on for.

"How'd we get on this subject anyway?" she asks after a long silence.

With Lauren, silence is always comfortable. Neither of us feels the need to fill the void with pointless chatter. Our friendship is like a well-oiled machine, except in the bedroom, where it all fell apart the one time we tried to take this flirtation-slash-slow-burn-slash-unful-filled-desire-that-is-ever-present between us to the next level.

How do you spell d-i-s-a-s-t-e-r?

Until that night six months ago, I hadn't known it was possible to do sex *wrong*. I don't like to brag, but the word "god" has often been used regarding my abilities between the sheets. Until I took Lauren to bed, I'd been the recipient of an endless streak of five-star reviews on my performance. But lo and behold, it's actually possible to get it so wrong you aren't sure if you'll ever again be able to look at the woman you've lusted after for years—while telling yourself you're "just" friends —in the aftermath of such calamity.

"I have no idea how we got on this subject," I reply as I shake off the disturbing memories.

"We were talking about orgasms," she reminds me.

The word "orgasms" reminds me of the dreadful encounter that threw a bucket of ice on our longtime slow burn for each other. There were no orgasms that night. "*You're* talking orgasms. I'm trying to eat my wings." Thank God we were able to salvage the friendship that means so much to both of us, not to mention our group of mutual friends.

Her best friend, Honey, got together with my close friend Blake last year, and they'd love to see us together, too. That isn't going to happen, but beer and wings on Mondays? That happens every week without fail. If I find myself living for Monday, well...

She laughs at my comment about trying to eat my wings. I love the sound of her laugh. There's something earthy and sexy and dirty about it. In truth, I love everything about her. I love the curly blonde hair that would look messy on another woman but suits her to perfection. I love her big brown eyes and how she's so honest that when she tries to lie about anything, she cries. I love that she spends as much time at the gym as I do and has the biceps to prove it. I adore the piercings that line her left ear and the butterfly tattoos that covers scars we never talk about on her inner wrists.

She loves butterflies. They're all over her house and the flower shop that she owns in town. They're sort of her trademark, along with the bright colors that decorate her and her surroundings. Tonight she's wearing a frilly orange top with white short-shorts. Not that I noticed her awesome legs and ass on the way in or anything...

The other thing I absolutely love about her is the way she looks at me as if I'm the guy she'd want if she could have her pick of all the men in the world. If I were looking for a forever kind of woman, Lauren would be at the top of my list of candidates. In fact, she'd be the only candidate. But the last thing I want, after years of endless responsibility, is a serious relationship or anything that would permanently tie me to Marfa. She owns a home and a business here. Getting involved with Lauren on a more serious level than as best friends would definitely tie me to Marfa, and that's my biggest hesitation where she's concerned.

"Sometimes, I think it's me," she says softly. "Like there's something wrong with me."

This stuns me even more than hearing Wayne fucking Peterson was the first guy to make her come. "What do you mean?"

She looks so defeated that I want to reach across the table to offer comfort, but I can't seem to move my arms or anything else for that matter. "When a girl starts to string together enough disastrous sexual encounters, she begins to wonder if *she's* the problem."

"That's ridiculous. It's not *you*. You're just picking the wrong guys."

She gives me a look filled with skepticism. "Including you?"

I'm riveted by the first mention either of us has made of that awful night when everything that could go wrong did. "That was an off night, and it was more my fault than yours."

She sweeps away my comment with her hand. "You're just saying that because you're a good friend, and you're trying to make me feel better."

"That is *not* why I said it, and it *was* my fault."

"Why do you think that?" she asks, looking adorably perplexed.

I've given this a lot of thought in the months that have passed since that night, and I've come to some conclusions. "First of all, I was freaked out about ruining our friendship, which messed with my head. Both of them, actually. Second, we did it all wrong."

"There's a *wrong* way?" she asks, her brows rising in amazement.

"Hell yes, there's a wrong way. We rushed over the preliminaries. I didn't take my time. I got naked with you five minutes after the first time I kissed you. That's not how it should be done when two people have as much history between them as we do."

The truth of the matter is I'd wanted her naked and horizontal in a bed with me for so long that when opportunity knocked the first time, I pounced like a hormonal teenage boy rather than the experienced man that I am. I've sorely regretted that ever since—even more so now that I know she's been blaming herself. "It shouldn't have happened that way. You deserve so much better than what you got from me. I think you are..."

"What?" she asks again in that sweet, sexy tone. "What am I?"

"You're *everything*," I whisper gruffly.

"Except compatible with you in bed," she reminds me with the kind of bluntness I expect from her. We talk about *everything*. See Exhibit A above—orgasms.

I clear my throat and decide to take a dive that's been six long, torturous months in the making, since the ill-fated night with her put a serious hit on my sexual GPA. "I really think we ought to try again." I actually hadn't had that thought until I heard that she thinks she's the problem. I absolutely can't have her thinking that when it's not true. Before I pick up stakes and head out of this godforsaken town, I need to prove otherwise to her, if it's the last thing I do.

Before the words are even all the way out of my mouth, her head is shaking—and not in a good way. "I can't bear to be humiliated like that again."

"I like to think we were equally humiliated, and at the end of the day, it's just me and you here, Lauren."

"And maybe we're better as best friends."

"I'm not ready to accept that after one failed attempt."

"*Garrett*..." The pleading edge to her voice makes me feel like an ass for forcing her to talk about it. "We were so lucky to get past that and to put this back on track." She gestures to the plate of wings and the bottles of beer on the table.

Forgetting where we are and that half the town is probably watching, I reach across the table for her hand. I need to touch her. For the longest time, she's been the brightest light in my life. Why? I can't say exactly. Except for the one night we tried to have more, we've only ever been the best of friends. All I know is that I can't leave her with any thoughts of her own inadequacy—especially if I've contributed to them in any way. "Give me one week to prove it's not you. That's all I'm asking."

"But what if we really are better off as friends than..."

"Lovers?"

She cringes and wrinkles her cute little nose. "That's such a gross word."

Laughing, I say, "What would you call it?"

"Friends with benefits?"

"I can live with that description. I want another chance, Lauren. Let me show you what can happen when we savor rather than devour."

She draws in a shaky-sounding deep breath, and her face flushes with a rosy glow that has my cock stirring.

"What do you say?"

She takes a drink from her beer bottle. Even that seems insanely sexy in light of our conversation. "How would it work, this so-called week where you prove it's not me?" Is her voice huskier than usual, or is that wishful thinking on my part?

I've thought about what went wrong that night from every possible angle, and I've realized that a longer, more drawn-out seduction is what we should've done then—and it's what we'll do this time, if she gives me another chance. "You'd have to trust me with the details. I wouldn't want you to worry about anything. Leave it all to me."

"Under one condition."

"Name it."

"No matter what happens, you promise me we'll still have this after." Again, she gestures to the wings and beers, acting as a metaphor for our friendship.

"You have my word. Do I have yours?" I want her to know the friendship is as important to me as it is to her. "No matter what happens, we still have this?"

"Absolutely."

"Is that a yes, then?"

She nods. "I'm willing to try again if you're so sure it won't be another disaster."

I'm not sure of anything other than I want another chance. "Tomorrow night, I'll pick you up at seven. I want you to wear the sexiest dress you own with nothing under it. Oh, and heels. I want some sky-high heels, too. Can you do that?"

Her mouth drops open in shock. I can't wait to see those plump lips wrapped around my cock. We didn't get to that the first time around. We'll definitely get there next time. "Lauren?"

"Um, yes, okay. I can do that."

I signal for our check, throw a fifty on it and stand to leave. We came separately, but next time, we'll come together. I almost laugh at my own joke. Bending, I brush a kiss over her rosy cheek. "See you tomorrow."

After I leave her, I wonder how long she sat there with her mouth hanging open over my audacious instructions. I can't wait for tomorrow night.

I have a confession to make. I fucking hate Marfa. Sure, it was an okay place to grow up, but it was never my plan to be stuck in the middle of buttfuck nowhere West Texas as an adult. We're three hours to El Paso to the west, five, six and eight hours respectively to San Antonio, Austin and Houston to the east, and seven and a half hours to Dallas to the north. In short, Marfa is next to nothing but wide-open desert.

I went to college at Texas A&M, eight hours from Marfa in College Station, between Austin and Houston, and spent many a wild weekend in both cities. At the end of my senior year, I was entertaining job offers in several big Texas cities when the unthinkable happened. My dad dropped dead at work.

He was so proud of me for following him into accounting and boasted of my three-point-nine GPA to all his colleagues. We were consulting daily about the job offers I'd received and had narrowed it down to an oil company and a *Fortune* 500 corporation with offices all over the world. The plan was to start "local," meaning anywhere in Texas, and end up somewhere awesome. Dad was pushing me in the corporate direction over the always-volatile oil industry.

Until one night he didn't come home from work on time, and my mom went looking for him. She found him hunched over his desk, his body already cold and rigid. An autopsy determined he'd been dead about three hours by the time she found him.

Just that quickly, my plans changed, and all my choices were taken from me along with the father I worshipped. I did what was expected —and desperately needed—by coming home to run my father's local accounting business, the same business that supported my mom and the three younger siblings who were heading to college in the next few years.

This is one of many reasons I resent my older brother, who has been more than happy to leave all the responsibility for our family to good old Garrett while he and his wife, Debbie, have the time of their lives in California, or so it seems to me from the pictures they post constantly on Facebook. Every one of those pictures made me want to rip his face off for the first couple of years after my dad died, until I decided to let go of the bitterness that was eating me up inside. It wasn't Tommy's fault that our father died, or that I was the most qualified to take over the family business. At least, that's what I tell myself so I won't actually murder him on one of his infrequent visits.

Six years later, I've gotten an MBA through an online program and tripled the annual gross revenue of my father's small-town practice. I act as chief financial officer and/or controller for most of the major businesses in town. Ever since my father died, I've had the same plan— get my younger siblings through college, set my mom up for retire- ment, sell the business to some enterprising CPA looking to step into a successful practice, and then *finally* go see to the plans that were put on hold for six long years.

Last year, my staff of seven and I cleared a million dollars in net revenue. For the non-accountants out there, that's *after* expenses. That cool million means I have the tuition I need for my sisters and can set my mom up royally. This week I got a phone call from a headhunter I've been working with for a year as I test the waters to see what else might be out there for me now that I've fulfilled my obligations to my family. He's set up an interview with a huge tech company in Austin for the end of next week, and he said they want me bad. It sure does feel good to be wanted.

I'd be on my way out of Marfa forever if it wasn't for one small, niggling detail named Lauren Davies, who also happens to own one of the few businesses in Marfa that *doesn't* use the services of Garrett McKinley, CPA.

I've had my theories as to why, theories that were confirmed on that one ill-fated night we spent in her bed in which everything that could go wrong did. She confessed that the chemistry that's always simmered on a low boil between us stopped her from hiring me to handle her accounting. Turns out, that was probably a savvy move on her part, because the first time we decided to test that chemistry in the lab, so to speak, we created a disaster of epic proportions. I shudder thinking about my first-ever case of performance anxiety that led to one fumbling attempt after another to successfully close the deal.

Ugh. I can't bear to remember it. Except... One shining memory stands out in a sea of things I'd rather forget—the visual of Lauren's spectacular naked body that is so seared into my brain it'll never be forgotten.

As I sit in the office in the much larger building I moved the business to three years after dad died, visions of naked Lauren dance like sugarplums through my addled brain, especially after last night's conversation about orgasms. Thinking about giving her an orgasm has me hard as concrete *in my office, in the middle of the freaking workday*.

If I made a spreadsheet of Lauren's attributes, it would look something like this:

1. Smooth, lightly tanned skin.
2. Big, full breasts with light brown nipples made for sucking.
3. A flat, toned belly.
4. Endless, sexy legs.
5. A completely bare pussy (or as I like to think of it—the frosting on a delicious piece of cake).
6. A perfect ass that makes me want to grab on and do dirty, dirty things.

7. Gorgeous brown eyes.
8. Curly blonde hair that I want to wrap around my hands when I fuck her from behind.
9. A mouth made for sin, and I have a few specific sins in mind when it comes to her luscious mouth.

Total = Perfection.

I lick my lips as I catalog every spectacular detail of her stunning body. Of course, I've always known she's hot as fuck. We grew up together. I've seen her in everything from a bikini to a prom gown to the shortest of skirts and the highest of heels. But seeing her in absolutely nothing was a revelation. Literally. And figuratively. I'm never sure of the proper use of those two words, so let me sum it up—Lauren Davies is a literal and figurative smoking-hot babe.

Tonight I'm going to prove to her that her challenges with guys have nothing at all to do with her and everything to do with *them*. Once I get her feeling better about herself, I'm so outta here.

Sex God is available in print from *Amazon.com* and other online retailers, or you can purchase a signed copy from Marie's store at *shop.marieforce.com*.

ALSO BY MARIE FORCE

Contemporary Romances Available from Marie Force

The Gansett Island Series

Book 1: Maid for Love *(Mac & Maddie)*

Book 2: Fool for Love *(Joe & Janey)*

Book 3: Ready for Love *(Luke & Sydney)*

Book 4: Falling for Love *(Grant & Stephanie)*

Book 5: Hoping for Love *(Evan & Grace)*

Book 6: Season for Love *(Owen & Laura)*

Book 7: Longing for Love *(Blaine & Tiffany)*

Book 8: Waiting for Love *(Adam & Abby)*

Book 9: Time for Love *(David & Daisy)*

Book 10: Meant for Love *(Jenny & Alex)*

Book 10.5: Chance for Love, *A Gansett Island Novella (Jared & Lizzie)*

Book 11: Gansett After Dark *(Owen & Laura)*

Book 12: Kisses After Dark *(Shane & Katie)*

Book 13: Love After Dark *(Paul & Hope)*

Book 14: Celebration After Dark *(Big Mac & Linda)*

Book 15: Desire After Dark *(Slim & Erin)*

Book 16: Light After Dark *(Mallory & Quinn)*

Book 17: Victoria & Shannon (Episode 1)

Book 18: Kevin & Chelsea (Episode 2)

A Gansett Island Christmas Novella

Book 19: Mine After Dark *(Riley & Nikki)*

Book 20: Yours After Dark *(Finn & Chloe)*

Book 21: Trouble After Dark *(Deacon & Julia)*

Book 22: Rescue After Dark *(Mason & Jordan)*

Book 23: Blackout After Dark

The Green Mountain Series

Book 1: All You Need Is Love *(Will & Cameron)*

Book 2: I Want to Hold Your Hand *(Nolan & Hannah)*

Book 3: I Saw Her Standing There *(Colton & Lucy)*

Book 4: And I Love Her *(Hunter & Megan)*

Novella: You'll Be Mine *(Will & Cam's Wedding)*

Book 5: It's Only Love *(Gavin & Ella)*

Book 6: Ain't She Sweet *(Tyler & Charlotte)*

The Butler, Vermont Series

(Continuation of Green Mountain)

Book 1: Every Little Thing *(Grayson & Emma)*

Book 2: Can't Buy Me Love *(Mary & Patrick)*

Book 3: Here Comes the Sun *(Wade & Mia)*

Book 4: Till There Was You *(Lucas & Dani)*

Book 5: All My Loving *(Landon & Amanda)*

Book 6: Let It Be *(Lincoln & Molly)*

Book 7: Come Together *(Noah & Brianna)*

The Treading Water Series

Book 1: Treading Water

Book 2: Marking Time

Book 3: Starting Over

Book 4: Coming Home

Book 5: Finding Forever

The Miami Nights Series

Book 1: How Much I Feel *(Carmen & Jason)*

Book 2: How Much I Care *(Maria & Austin)*

Book 3: How Much I Love *(Dee's story)*

Single Titles

Five Years Gone

One Year Home

Sex Machine

Sex God

Georgia on My Mind

True North

The Fall

The Wreck

Love at First Flight

Everyone Loves a Hero

Line of Scrimmage

The Quantum Series

Book 1: Virtuous *(Flynn & Natalie)*

Book 2: Valorous *(Flynn & Natalie)*

Book 3: Victorious *(Flynn & Natalie)*

Book 4: Rapturous *(Addie & Hayden)*

Book 5: Ravenous *(Jasper & Ellie)*

Book 6: Delirious *(Kristian & Aileen)*

Book 7: Outrageous *(Emmett & Leah)*

Book 8: Famous *(Marlowe & Sebastian)*

Romantic Suspense Novels Available from Marie Force

The Fatal Series

One Night With You, *A Fatal Series Prequel Novella*

Book 1: Fatal Affair

Book 2: Fatal Justice

Book 3: Fatal Consequences

Book 3.5: Fatal Destiny, *the Wedding Novella*

Book 4: Fatal Flaw

Book 5: Fatal Deception

Book 6: Fatal Mistake

Book 7: Fatal Jeopardy

Book 8: Fatal Scandal

Book 9: Fatal Frenzy

Book 10: Fatal Identity

Book 11: Fatal Threat

Book 12: Fatal Chaos

Book 13: Fatal Invasion

Book 14: Fatal Reckoning

Book 15: Fatal Accusation

Book 16: Fatal Fraud

Historical Romance Available from Marie Force

The Gilded Series
Book 1: Duchess by Deception

Book 2: Deceived by Desire

ABOUT THE AUTHOR

Marie Force is the *New York Times* best-selling author of contemporary romance, romantic suspense and erotic romance. Her series include Gansett Island, Fatal, Treading Water, Butler Vermont, Quantum and Miami Nights.

Her books have sold more than 10 million copies worldwide, have been translated into more than a dozen languages and have appeared on the *New York Times* bestseller more than 30 times. She is also a *USA Today* and *Wall Street Journal* bestseller, as well as a Speigel bestseller in Germany.

Her goals in life are simple—to finish raising two happy, healthy, productive young adults, to keep writing books for as long as she possibly can and to never be on a flight that makes the news.

Join Marie's mailing list on her website at *marieforce.com* for news about new books and upcoming appearances in your area. Follow her on Facebook at *www.Facebook.com/MarieForceAuthor* and on Instagram at *www.instagram.com/marieforceauthor/*. Contact Marie at *marie@marieforce.com*.